The Tales of Alexandria Stecklar
The Locket

The Tales of Alexandria Stecklar
The Locket

By
Tiara J. Brown

The Tales of Alexandria Stecklar: The Locket

Copyright © 2022 Tiara Brown.

All rights reserved.

First edition.

No part of this story may be used or reproduced in any manner whatsoever without written permission except in the case of brief quotations embodied in critical articles or reviews.

This story is a work of fiction. Names, characters, places, and incidents are either from the author's imagination or are being used fictitiously. Any resemblance to actual persons, living or dead, events or locales is purely coincidental.

The publisher is not responsible for websites (or their content) that are not owned by the publisher.

ISBN: 979-8-9861355-0-2 (hardcover)
ISBN: 979-8-9861355-1-9 (paperback)
ISBN: 979-8-9861355-2-6 (ebook)

Visit the author's website at www.tiarajbrown.com.

Book format & cover designed by Ebook Launch.

Map designed by Najla Kay

Photography by my friend, Alli.

Edited by Jenny Bowman and Matthew R. Bishop.

Printed in the United States of America.

FOR MY FRIENDS AND FAMILY

Thank you so much for supporting me throughout my writing journey. I thank God that you are all in my life. I am truly blessed to know each and every one of you.

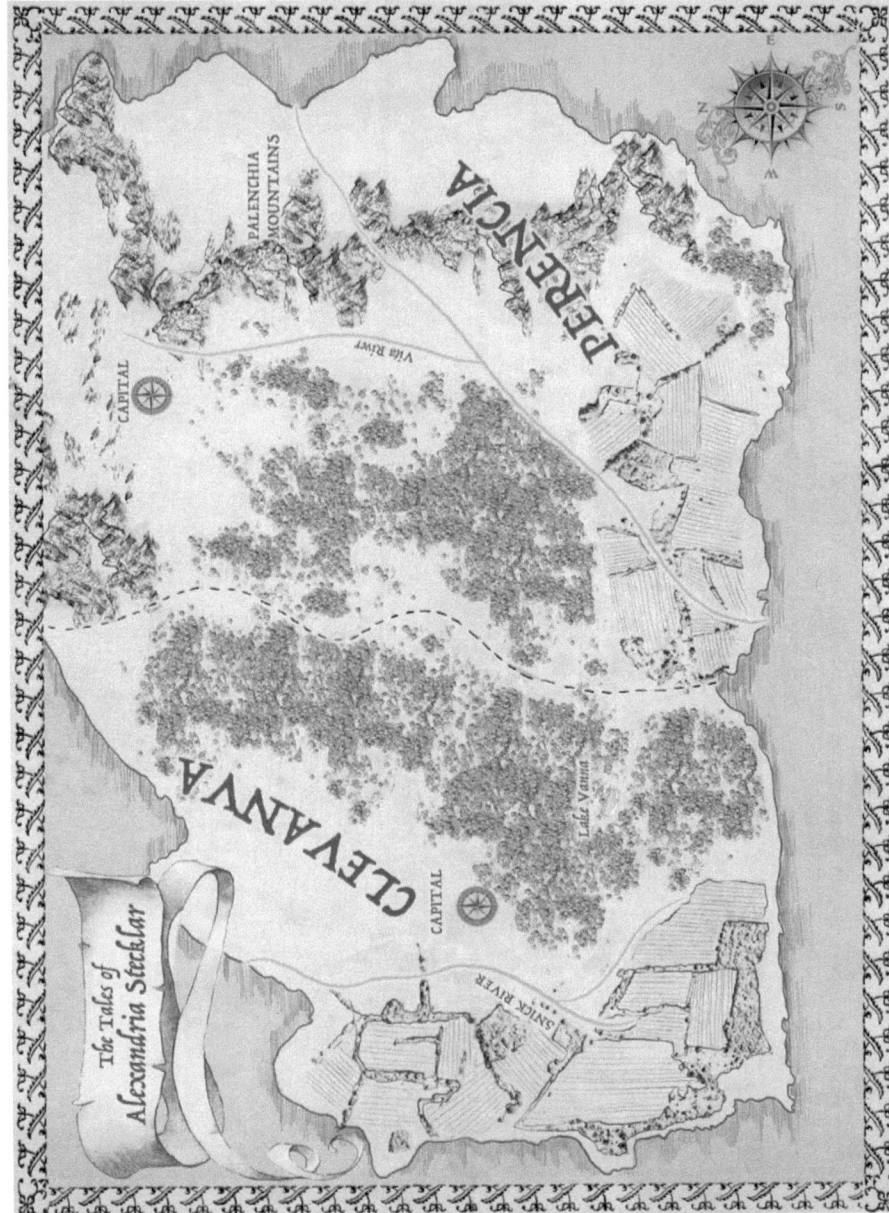

PROLOGUE

Hatred. War. Death. Pain. No matter how hard we try, it seems as if Man cannot escape these casualties, and no matter how hard I try, neither can I.

It is the opening of my favorite book, "The Knight Chronicles: The Stag Versus the Lion." Although, I do admit that it is a bit dramatic.

"Ow."

Speaking of which…

"My deepest apologies, Your Grace." Isabelle, one of my maids, has just stuck me with a needle while sewing it in and out of the seam of the right sleeve of my dress.

"It's fine. Trust me. I've been through a lot worse." I smile in assurance.

In fact, the letters laced between my fingers remind me of those times. I have read them over and over again, melting them into my memory. They are the words of my sister, my father, and the once-held prisoner. They accompany my thoughts and fill in the holes that I did not witness. I suppose that I will take them or any excuse to distract me from the now.

I used to survive on the tales of ancient dynasties, the trials and tribulations of kings and queens, and even the journeys of young stable boys as they embark on their quests for adventure. I was held captive by nearly every word. Yet, as exciting as these stories were to read about, it was an entirely different experience to live through them.

As Isabelle continues to sew, my eyes gaze up from the three letters and examine the walls along the room. In painting after painting after painting of whom I assume are my ancestors, are past monarchs sit on their thrones to receive the crown. All are nicely framed. They are decorated with gold cherubs, and the outlines of roses are carved into them.

Their subjects never smile or frown. Instead, they only hold cold, hard gazes that pierce right through me.

I close my eyes and take a deep breath. Despite all attempts, my body still shakes. I open my eyes, and stare at the reflection before me in a long glass mirror.

Huh. It's actually kind of ironic, isn't it? This is not how I ever envisioned myself. I hardly even recognize the girl standing in the mirror. She is young and already raised on a platform. Her dress is laced with golden thread and trimmings that match the color of her eyes. She bares hair as black as ink that has been curled and pinned, half up and half down, which touches past her shoulders. Her complexion is a bit tanner than it used to be. Even her shoes are different. Instead of brown worn boots, she wears sliver slippers that sparkle in the light.

She tries to stand tall, despite the gravity of obligations that she is about to take on. Despite the consequences that will come and the weight that they will carry. Like all monarchs, she is expected to be firm but fair, aloof yet affable, and above all – strong.

However, how can she? Especially when she herself is still just a child in so many ways. A young spirit that doesn't hesitate to talk back to authority, yet still feels the urge to flee when she's scared. Of course, she would never be caught dead in a gown such as this; beautiful and elegant that she has grown to love.

Hmm. Now, I know what you must be thinking. *You, ungrateful, little brat. Most would kill for a life such as this, and here you are complaining about it.*

Yes, I am very fortunate, and while I do not disregard that, this is still not the life that I fought for, nor is it the life that I would have ever chosen for myself. It is the life that I was given, and the life that I should be most honored to have. Yet, it has been the life that has caused me the most pain, the most regret, and above all the most guilt.

"Your Grace." Mildred, my other maid, approaches me with a plain wooden jewelry box. She curtseys before me and opens the box.

"May I?" she asks.

Inside is a tiny heart-shaped silver locket. The front of the locket had been broken off years ago, and only the back and the chain remain.

I nod and move my hair out of the way.

She stands up and places the box on a stand beside her. Gently, her hands pick up the locket. She walks behind me and slowly places its chain around my neck. My neck shivers from the icy impact of the chain, while the body of the locket nearly burns into my chest.

My fingers slowly graze across its body.

"Promise me." A haunting whisper echoes into my ears.

The locket further reminds me of that day. It was six years ago, yet it still seems as if it were only a few days ago. As if all of this is a dream that I am waiting to wake up from. I tightly grip the locket into my palm and look back up at the portraits. I meet their eyes with mine. "You were born for this," they say.

Click!

A gust of cold air presses against my back.

"Her Majesty, please welcome, Lord William Edgewater," a herald roars from the corridor.

My maids' curtesy and step back towards the wall.

I turn to face Lord Edgewater.

He is a nobleman in the High Council. Tall and heavy set, he is a cheery fellow. The thin hair on top of his head, along with his thick, coarse beard and mustache, reside in dark brown and gray spiraled curls. His robes are always groomed with never a button or collar out of place.

"Your Grace," Lord Edgewater bows, then quickly rises. "they are ready for you now."

Once again, I take a deep breath and glance back at my reflection.

It is time.

My eyes close, attempting to calm the sound of my beating heart as it pulses through my ears. I exhale. My hands clutch the fabric of the gown around my stomach. I hear Lord Edgewater proclaim the words, "Long may the legend and tale of your reign begin."

And with those words, I smirk.

Huh. My tale. My reign. The truth is this is not the start of my tale. No. My story began a long time ago. But let's not get too ahead of ourselves. I will get to that part of the tale in due time. Now, bare with me. I recall all of the events that I have witnessed as clear and as bright as the noon-day sun. However, as I have said earlier, all of the events that I did not bare witness to are all written down in these letters that I still hold in my hand. Are they accurate? I don't know. Maybe. I guess, one day we will find out.

Until then, let's see. I will start the tale those six years ago when I just fifteen, for that is when my journey truly began…

ALEXANDRIA

PROMISE ME

"Alex," I heard the faint whisper inside my head as I laid still on a soft heap of grass. My skin was comforted by the warm, lightweight fabric of my soft gray sweater. I was surrounded by colors of red, yellow, and orange in the trees, and spread across the ground were tiny brown leaves stippled throughout the array of colors. The brown leaves matched some tree trunks, while others were strikingly white with oval patches of dark brown and black. The forest was filled with the chatter of squirrels scurrying up the trees, and the chirps and flutters of birds as they leapt off the branches and flew into the sky.

"Alex." I heard the voice again. It was louder, but I continued to ignore it.

I closed my eyes. The warm kiss of the sun seeped its rays through the leaves of the trees and onto my face. The autumn breeze danced through my long hair and the scent of ferns and pine cones filled my senses. It was utter bliss.

"Alex!"

"What!?" I asked.

Frightened, I quickly opened my eyes. I stretched my arms out in front of me and levitated my freckled face and auburn-locked older sister, Hannah above me.

"Whoa," she yelped.

"Hannah!" I said.

She chuckled. "Well, hello to you too. Nice reflexes."

With telekinesis, I put her down as I sat up. "You scared the Hell out of me!"

"I do tend to have that effect on people." She grinned.

"It's not funny." I laced my fingers through the hair on the top of my head. "I thought we agreed that you wouldn't go into my thoughts anymore."

I sunk my face into my knees and tried to catch my breath as my heart sped. Unlike most people, I was cursed with a telepathic sister. Then again, I also didn't know most people. Huh.

"We did, but we also recall a certain agreement in which you said that you would stop sneaking out, so I would say that you broke that contract." She bent down beside me.

I gazed up at a tall thick oak tree and watched a bird flutter its wings as it was about to leap out of its nest.

"Hey! Alex!" Hannah snapped her fingers inches from my nose. "Back down here."

"Wait, what!?" I asked as I shook my head back to reality.

"Great, now that I have your attention. What are you even doing out here?" Hannah asked.

"Does it matter?" I turned my head away.

Hannah stood back up. I could see her still staring at me at the corner of my eye.

"Gee, I don't know. Let's see." Hannah's voice remained lighthearted, yet her hands went to her hips. "You are lying down outside in the middle of the woods in the middle of a warzone and ya know…hmm… that doesn't seem the least bit odd to you?"

"First of all, you are exaggerating. Second, no one comes here. And third—" I turned my head to face her. "Don't pretend to be more worried than you actually are."

Her face turned stern. She crossed her arms.

"You are going to get yourself killed," she said.

"Uh huh," I said in disbelief.

"Ugh. You're so selfish sometimes. Do you even care that you're also risking the lives of myself, Mom, and Dad?"

"Oh, yeah. Don't want to upset Mom and Dad," I said, sarcastically.

"If they catch you—"

"Then, what?" I interrupted. "They'll keep me in a hole? Oh wait, they already do that."

Hannah rolled her eyes.

"So, damn dramatic." Hannah looked around at the ground, the trees, and the bushes. "I don't even understand why you like coming out here so much." Her nose crinkled at their scent. "At least all of the bugs will die off soon when winter comes."

She swatted at some invisible insect that hadn't even appeared yet.

I rolled my eyes and said, "It's not my fault that you hate freedom."

"And, its not my fault that you would rather be dead than safe."

"And she calls me dramatic," I mumbled. I stood up and turned away from Hannah. I leapt onto a large log, stretched my arms out for balance, and began to walk across. "Besides, last time I checked, alone time isn't actually a crime."

"It should be, considering your recklessness," she said.

I jumped off the log and looked back at her. "You have no idea what it's like to live with people that can constantly read your mind, especially when you have the power to block it out."

"You give me too much credit. My gift isn't as strong as Dad's. You really think that he can't read my mind too?" she asked.

I only stared at Hannah.

Her face relaxed. "Look, I'm not saying that everything that Mom and Dad do is right, but you know as well as I do that, they are only just trying to protect us. They're doing their best and yeah, it is rare, but others have come through this forest before. The last thing you want is to be here when they find you."

She extended her hand out towards me.

I paused.

I stared at Hannah. She stared back at me with her head titled and her big brown puppy-dog eyes, pouting. I hated when she would do this. Aside from moments like these, she was always the good kid. The kid that always did what she was told, the first born by two years, and of course the one that my parents always wanted. She was even elegant like our mother. They both held such grace when they walked that I was never ever able to fully imitate. Yet, at times Hannah also carried a certain sternness that she had clearly gotten from our father.

She bought into their hysteria, while I questioned it. I was the weird one, the difficult one. And thus, the one that was always treated differently.

"Fine." I sighed. "I know that all they want is to protect us."

Reluctantly, I walked towards Hannah. She put her arm around me and said, "That always does work on you, now doesn't it? Come on, let's go."

We walked further between the trees, until we came to our stop. To others, it was a random spot in middle of these woods, but to us it was home. Hannah bent down onto her knees with her face towards the ground. A small yellow light shot from the ground and scanned the retina of her eyes. She stood back up, and we both took a step back. A small crevice in the ground opened in the shape of a square. We walked down the hole and on to a steel staircase. Once our heads disappeared, the opening shut.

We continued down the staircase until we reached a dead end. Another yellow light shot from each of the walls and scanned our entire bodies. The wall in front of us opened, and in its place were a second set of declining stairs. We walked down the second staircase, the wall behind us silently closing.

To my discontent, we were prisoners to the repercussions of a war between technology and magic: Our kingdom of Clevanva against our neighbor, the kingdom of Perencia. We were psychics and they were sorcerers. We thrived in our advances in computers, weaponry, and security, while they sullied themselves backwards in magic.

Fair and just were we under the watchful eye of the Stanburg Clan in our benevolent constitutional monarchy. Yet, iniquitous and cruel were the sorcerers under the dictatorship that they called an absolute monarchy, coining them "The Wicked" or "The Wics" for short. Or at least, that is what the history books said. Nonetheless, when they attacked our nation, our people were left with two options: Either to join the war efforts or to run. Our family chose the latter. We lived underground on the border, shrouded by a forest. We rarely came up for anything, except when food or water became scarce. Well, at least my parents did anyway. Hannah and I were always kept under strict lock and key.

The door opened, and we entered into our living room from the bottom of the stairs. Our home was rectangular. The solid steel walls held multiple black surveillance screens. Charcoaled sketches ranged from simple shapes such as squares to intricate portraits of Hannah, Dad, and myself peppered in between, and one large colored family painting hung on the back wall in the living room.

In the portrait stood Mom and Dad in the back and Hannah and I in the front. Most of Mom's hair was bright auburn with a few highlighted strands of light caramel placed backed into her usual bun. She had full, wavy bangs that fell over her forehead and along the sides of her face. Her sweater was black, with shadings of gray to enhance its intricate threaded details, and the bottom of her ears glowed yellow from the earrings that she had painted. She even added the elegant freckles along her pale face. Dad called them stars.

Same as Mom, Dad also wore a black sweater with shading of gray to enhance and show the differences of the sweater. He wore thin-rimmed gold glasses, and his chestnut brown hair was cut short as always. He stood a half foot taller than Mom. His hand rested on her side.

Hannah and I stood right next to each other. She was ten years old, and I was eight. Her hair was pulled back into a high ponytail, with the mane of her locks flowing a little past her shoulders. She proudly showed the stars along her pale face, along with a grin that reached ear to ear. She wore a short-sleeved, simple pink dress that met her knees and white socks. I, on the other hand, wore my black mane down in a low ponytail. It also stretched past my shoulders. Like Mom, I wore my usual bangs. Yet, unlike Mom, mine were parted down the middle. They fell straight and long along on the sides of my face. Similar to Hannah, I was in a simple dress that met my knees, and I wore white socks. However, my dress was purple. And although I was also smiling, it was not as big of a grin as Hannah's.

We were a slender family in that painting, and still we remained just as slender.

Hannah stepped in front of me. We looked to the right into the kitchen. There was not a soul. There was only the countertop, refrigerator, stove, and cabinets.

We looked to the left in the hallway. The last door at the very end was our bedroom. "Now!" Hannah whispered.

Quickly, we dashed to the left. However, stepping in front of us from around the corner was our mother, Gabrielle Stecklar. "And, where exactly have you girls been?" she asked.

Her hair still mirrored the portrait. Yet, her eyes did not bare resemblance to the painting. Instead, they narrowed in on us.

"Um, nowhere, Mom. Just hanging out. Girl stuff," Hannah said.

"Really?" Mom crossed her arms. "Is that why you were running?"

In unison, Hannah and I both said, "Yes."

"They're lying."

A voice echoed from the one of the couches. Our father, Richard Stecklar, sat up from the couch cushions, with his ruffled hair and his brown eyes glaring at me.

"They were outside again." Dad stood up.

"Alex!" Mom said.

"But, I wasn't thinking about—" I began. However, I stopped and looked over at my sister. "Hannah!"

"Sorry, I got nervous. I told you I'm not as strong as Dad," Hannah said.

"Ugh, my gosh," I mumbled.

"What am I going to do with the both of you!? Hannah, you are my eldest, and it's time that you start acting like it! Running around with your sister's antics—" Mom said.

"But, Mom—" Hannah began.

Mom cut her off. "I don't want to hear it!" She turned towards me. "And, Alex—"

"Sorry, I don't like being a hostage in my own home," I mumbled, staring off to the side.

"Watch your mouth," Dad warned. He walked over to me, casting his shadow over Hannah and I. "We are in the middle of a war. Do you understand?"

"Dad, wait!" Hannah stepped in front of me.

He stopped.

"It was actually me. Not Alex. It was my fault," Hannah said. Her voice held both a hint of a quiver, but also conviction at the same time.

I looked up at the back of Hannah's head.

Our mother looked at our father and back at us. Dad only stared at Hannah. "Hannah, are you sure?" Mom asked.

"I'm also cooped up in here. It was both my idea and my doing. If you have to yell at someone, yell at me," Hannah said.

"Is that so?" Dad asked.

Hannah nodded, 'yes.'

"Hannah, you are an excellent student. I have taught you well, but have you forgotten that I am the one that taught you this technique? Creating false memories and emotional tactics will not convince me of your lie. Nice try," he said.

"But, Dad," Her voice broke the act.

"Go wait in the other room," he said.

"But—"

"Now!"

Hannah looked back at me and mouthed the words, 'sorry' before walking off as our father had ordered.

"As for you," he looked back at me. "Do you understand the consequences if someone had seen you? You are not only putting yourself in danger, but you are also risking the lives all of us! If some rogue sorcerer—"

"Richard—" Mom began.

My dad looked at her, cutting her off. "No, Gabby. Enough is enough!"

My nails dug into my hands at my side as my eyes turned red.

Dad continued, "Step outside again and—"

"And what? You'll lock me in the closest, again?"

"Worse. Especially if you ever want to see daylight, again. This is your final waring!"

I ran to my bedroom as my parents continued to talk.

"Richard, calm down!"

"No, this is getting ridiculous!"

In my room, I cracked the door to listen.

"She can't keep doing this, Gabby! She is going to get us killed!"

"Richard..."

I closed the door. I looked straight ahead. Gray walls; I was surrounded by gray walls. Tears streamed down my cheeks.

I ran over to the dresser. It stood against the wall in between twin beds. I told myself not to cry; that I couldn't cry as I searched for a box of tissue.

Grabbing the box, I accidentally knocked over a small framed picture of Hannah with our parents. She looked just like them, our mother's hair and our father's eyes. I looked up at my reflection in the large mirror that stood on the dresser. I had straight black hair and golden eyes. Even the shape of my eyes appeared to be different, sloping downward at a slightly different angle. My cheekbones were high while theirs were not. I suppose Dad and I had the same complexion. The only things that I had known for certain I had inherited from our mother were the small freckles that appeared along the sides of my nose and tops of cheeks when the sun kissed my skin.

"Gabby, you know how irrational she is! —"

I halted. I could still hear my dad shouting through the door. I cautiously walked towards it. I tangled my fingers into each other. Hesitating. Waiting.

I could listen. But what if he reads my mind and hears me? I was listening before, and he seemed too upset to notice. Maybe that would still apply?

"If anyone finds her or us —" he continued.

I took a deep breath and swallowed, attempting to stop the emerging formation of a knot in my throat. I pressed my ear against the door.

"I know. I know. But none of this is working," Mom said.

"She's not old enough. Maybe when the war is over—"

"If it's ever over! This war has been going on for more than ten years. When exactly do you expect it to end?"

"So you want to let our daughter risk the entire family?"

"That is not what I'm saying, and you know it!"

Their shouting had lowered into loud speech.

"I swear if she does this again—" I backed away from the door before I could hear the rest of Dad's sentence.

To my dismay, the knot in my throat grew larger. I would be trapped in this hole forever. My hands shook. I ran over to my bed. I laid down and buried my head in my pillow, as I finally allowed the tears to fall.

Oliver stood on top of the cliff, overlooking the horizon. The sky was a mixture of pink and blue that bled down to the red-plated, rooftops of the village beneath it. He stared down at the village. The chill breeze pricked his cheeks and the tip of his nose, while filling his nostrils with the scent of salted water. Seagulls squawked and squealed with chatter as they circled the shore in the air.

Oliver grinned.

Oh, how this town seems so different now. Oh, how everything was different and strange, he thought.

This village used to be his world and now it seemed so small. Although the faces had changed, the people were the same. He watched them converse with each other in the streets. Some pushed wagons, while others stood at the dock and pulled up the evening catch of fish with their large nets. He gazed towards the lighthouse. It was once a beacon of something so mysterious, something that filled the mind with fantasies of the world at sea and of other lands. Now, he only sighed. Was it relief? Was it disappointment? Maybe a mixture of both? He did not know.

His ears twitched at the sound of ruffling leaves behind him. Quick to his scabbard, he laced his fingers around the hilt of his sword. As he was about to turn around to face the threat, he heard the words: "You finally learned to use the damn thing. I suppose it's not too big for you, after all."

Oliver paused.

Oliver turned around. And there he was. The once-deranged old fool now stood tall, with fitted armor emblazoned with the mighty stag of his family's crest across his chest plate. His white hair was neatly combed and trimmed short. Tiny semi-circled peppered hairs covered his chin and nearly spread down to his neck. But what drew Oliver's eyes were the vertical pink scar from the tip of forehead down through his right eye and to his cheekbone, which had aged with the man.

Oliver nearly wept at the sight of him. "You're alive," he said, barely able to speak.

"Aye, and so are you," the knight's voice rasped.

Oliver took a step forward. "When the Orcs attacked…"

"I know." The knight held up his hand, Oliver quieted.

"But there will be time for that later. The Gramet Ship has been attacked and all of its booty has been stolen. Normally, His Majesty would never request the help of an amateur onion boy, but he did request the presence of the Golden Knight."

Oliver smiled.

"Then, the Golden Knight he shall have," he said.

The knight smiled briefly before burying the smile under his usual rough expression. "Well then, come now. We haven't got all day."

The knight turned and began to walk. Oliver glanced back at the little *village. He took a deep breath and whispered, "Goodbye old town." He turned back around, and walked forward into his next adventure.*

I closed the book, but let it remain levitating in front of me. It was late, and I was barefoot and in pajamas, sitting back on the couch in the dimly-lit living room. I closed my eyes, imagining the small village. As tiny as it felt to Oliver was equivalent to how big it felt to me. To see the shore, marketplaces, and people; what a small dream that the people in these books always took for granted. And then, to go on an adventure to see the oceans, mountains, and even deserts. One could only stare at four walls for so long. I wanted to go to the pictures and illustrations that I had seen from books, and at times manuals that my parents still kept. It was and still is one of my main joys.

In truth, it was the only privilege that my parents allowed. I snickered. Good thing Dad was a nerd. He encouraged reading and the gaining of any type of knowledge. My memory flashed with images of Dad coming home with a new book when I was little. Always used, never new. But I didn't care. My face would light up at the sight.

Everything was different, then. The books were once enough. Now, they only grew the craving to see the outside.

Curse this stupid war!
Curse my parents' delusions.

Very rarely were we ever alerted that someone was wandering above. More often than not, it was some animal walking or running through the forest. Maybe a deer, some rabbit, or once in a while a wolf. My parents' fear was irrational, but still my sister and I were victims of that irrationality.

A hand landed on my shoulder. I turned and grabbed its wrist. I opened my eyes to see Hannah.

"Only me," she said.

I let go of her wrist and asked, "What are you doing up so late?"

"Funny, I should be asking you the same question." She smirked and sat down beside me. "Also, I never asked you if you were alright after what happened today."

"Yeah, I'm fine. I always am," I lied. I leaned back and slightly off the side, resting my head on her shoulder. Hannah smiled and placed her arm around me.

She looked down at the book, *The Knight Chronicles: The Stag Versus the Lion,* and said, "This one again?"

"It's my favorite," I said.

"Clearly, with how many times you've read it. Better be careful, or else the binding is going to become undone."

"I'm sorry, is there somewhere else that you have to be?"

"I'm just saying that you can't put these types of books down, but you can't be bothered to read any of the books about our country's own history."

"Liking to read doesn't mean you like to read everything. Besides what's the point of reading about the rules of a world that you are not allowed to be part of?"

"So, you would rather read about things and stories that aren't real?"

"At least I am the one that actually reads."

"As if I don't have books too."

"Books on how to draw do not count."

"The pictures framed against these walls would disagree. Although I need to ask Mom or Dad when the next time they are going to sneak into town, again. My charcoal is running low."

Like our mother, Hannah was a born artist. All of the sketches that hung on the walls were their creations. Mom's specialty were the portraits of our family that ranged from different ages of us growing up to the occasional flower. Hannah's tastes, on the other hand, were a bit different. They were mostly random three-dimensional shapes or heavily detailed objects found around our home like lamps or dishes.

I bit my lip, unsure whether or not I should ask this next question. But ultimately, I decided. "Don't you think that it's strange how normal it is for Mom and Dad to go above ground and not for us?" I asked.

"What do you mean? It's always been like this. I've told you—"

"Yes, I've heard it a million times." I interrupted. "They are just trying to protect us. I get it. But Hannah, come on."

I sat up to face her and continued, "You're seventeen, and I'm fifteen. If they can be so calm and natural about it, then why can't we? It's not like we're kids anymore."

"Dad can only manipulate the minds of so many people at a time to make them see something else. And then to do that for all four of us at once, even he can't do that," Hannah said.

"Fine, he could just let one of us go with him and—"

"Alex, enough." Her voice turned stern.

"I'm just saying—"

"No," she interrupted. "We have to stay here where it's safe. When the time is right and they feel that we're ready—"

"Ugh, you don't know that," I said.

"They told me that."

"Well, they didn't tell me."

"Well, maybe if you stop sneaking out all of the time then they would. And what a better way to prove that one day you will be ready if you really want to get out so badly."

"Yay, so now you're on their side."

"Alex, I'm on your side. I've always been on your side. I just believe Mom and Dad are doing what they think is best."

"So, what do you think?" I asked.

"I think that—" She stopped. She pulled both her bottom and top lips inside her mouth and continued, "That you read too many fantasy stories, and it has polluted your mind."

Classic Hannah.

"You think I'm still a child." I leaned back into the couch and laid my head back on her shoulder.

"You act like one," she teased.

"Says the person that can't stay up past midnight," I teased.

"I swear you fall asleep early, once."

I laughed. "Once!? How about almost every time."

"Says the girl that still cuts the crust off her bread every time it has graced these quarters."

"It ruins the taste!"

"If you say so," Hannah chuckled.

"Well, it does. Don't act like I'm crazy for it."

"Mmm, you're the one who said it, not me," she said.

"You know what? You can leave."

"Yeah, here's the thing, I would, but apparently someone has to keep an eye on you." Hannah yawned.

I looked up her. Her eyes were half-shut.

"Seriously." My tone softened. "You can go to bed. It's okay."

"What, no. I can stay up and keep you company. It's fine." She yawned, again.

"I promise that I'm not going to run off in the middle of the night. This book is just way too good."

"Are you sure?"

"Yes."

I sat up straight and repositioned my back to lean only against the couch. Hannah slowly stood up. "Well, okay. I just wanted to make sure that you were alright. Enjoy your book, but don't stay up too late," she said.

"Thanks Mom," I said, sarcastically.

I opened the book and my nose went back into it while Hannah walked past me. Sneakily, she grabbed one of the couch pillows. "Night," she said.

"Night," I said.

Thump!

"Hey!" I turned to see that I was hit in the back of the head with a pillow, the same pillow that Hannah just had her arms. I grabbed it and threw it back at her.

"Ahhh!" Hannah laughed as she dodged it.

I rolled my eyes and faced forward. I levitated the book back to its place on the bookshelf. It was on the other side of the living room. On top of it laid a large golden globe that sat in a bronze circular stand with three legs; old, scratched and filled with scattered dents. And right above it was the family portrait.

My eyes lingered on the portrait.

"Everything was truly different."

I turned my attentions back to the book case. I gazed across the shelves. One by one, I pulled out different books, trying to decide what to read next. I had read every single one at least ten times. Well, almost every single one. On the end, left untouched and unread, was a corner of the shelf all on science, technology, and history (which I begrudged). And now, the history of...Ugh, who cares? I rolled my eyes.

Well, I supposed that I could give it a shot. It would be a funny and unexpected way to show up Hannah, especially if I formed a bet around it. It would surprise Dad, too. It was the one section of the bookshelf that I did not touch, except when forced to during history lessons.

Or, I really could just go to bed? Although the thought of showing up Hannah and surprising Dad made me smile, it did not matter. Nothing would change; not this home or my parents' perception of me.

I sighed. I looked up at the digital clock on the wall. It was a few minutes to midnight. I had not a drop of sleep in my eyes. History was boring. If I read a boring book, at least it could put me to sleep.

I looked back at the bookcase. Let's see, what was the most boring book on these shelves? *The History of Bacterial Diseases*? Nope. That sounded disgusting. *The History of Technology*? Nope. I didn't care. Ah. *The History of Plastic.* That sounded very boring, and would put me right to sleep.

I pointed my hand towards that book. But when trying to pull that one out, it wouldn't move.

"Well, that's weird."

I pulled harder, but still nothing.

My forehead creased with my confusion. I held both of my hands out in the air and pulled even harder. It wiggled, but refused to come out.

The Hell? I nearly shook my head in disbelief.

Wait. No. If I pulled too hard, I might rip or damage the book. However, the amount of force I was using should have beyond pulled it out. Was I getting rusty or tired?

No. This was ridiculous. *I'm telekinetic*, I reminded myself that *I'm basically, a professional mover.* I closed my eyes, took a deep breath, and concentrated. My arms tensed, and I clenched my jaw. The heels of my feet rose into the air. Soon, the balls of my feet and toes followed, hovering slightly off the floor. My arms began to tire and shake at the weight of lifting myself. I held as steady as I could, until I eventually fell to the floor and opened my eyes.

Ouch!

My hands went to my bum. I gazed around the room. Everything was still silent, and no one came out into the hall.

Good. No one heard me.

I suppose that answers my question.

I stood back up and shook off the fall from my limbs. I looked down at my palms. Weird. Not rusty. Not tired. I had been working on that self-levitation with Mom for months. If I was tried, I would not have been able to get a centimeter off the floor.

I extended my hands out again. I tightened my breath, and with my gift, I carefully directed all of my energy to the book. I felt its binding meticulously, as if I was physically holding it. I pulled. It was stuck. A corner of the binding was caught in something.

I walked over to the book. This much fuss over a book probably was not worth it. Yet, I couldn't let it go. I wrapped my fingers around the back binding of the hard-covered book. It was thick, and had a small gap between itself and the pages, showing its age. I pulled. It was starting to come out from the shelf.

Cht!

Crap! Something ripped. No! Put it back!

I shoved the book back in its original place with both hands and a little telekinesis, smacking it back into place. The book case hit the wall and shook.

Oops! Too hard!

The golden globe that sat on top of the book case in its stand began to rock.

"Don't," I whispered.

The globe moved back and forth.

"I swear." My eyes shifted with the globe, until it fell from its stand.

No! No! No!

Quickly, I stretched my palms out. With my gift, I stopped the globe in midair.

I sighed. "Good."

I levitated the globe back onto its stand. I checked the shelves. Everything looked as if they were in their rightful places. "Yup. My sign to go to bed."

I turned and began to walk away. When I reached the middle of the living room, my foot sunk into a hole that laid beneath the rug. I lifted my foot up. Our home was mostly steel. There should not be any holes in the floor. Strange. I set my foot down, back in the spot. Again, it slumped beneath the rest of the floor, creating a downward slope in the rug.

What? How was—?

I took a step back and I knelt down on my hands and knees. I placed one hand into the slope. "No floor," I whispered.

I got up and stepped off to the side. I glided my hands through the air, pushing back all of the furniture in the room at once. I gently pushed my hands forward, rolling up the rug and pushing it towards the couch. I gazed down. There it was, a small square opening in the floor.

My curiosity rose. I had never seen this before. It couldn't have been for some secret escape or attack plan if we were ever invaded. My parents would have at least told me about that. No, this had to be something else.

I bent down and reached inside it, pulling out a medium-sized wooden box. It was of worn oak, with lines of scratches scattered across it. The top of the box was attached with metal hinges on its back.

I opened it. Inside was a folded, dark blue blanket. My fingers ran across the blanket before I lifted it up into the air. It was heavy and soft. The blanket was small and square. There were a few strands of loose threads on its ends. However, overall the blanket was intact. I placed it on the floor beside me. I looked back inside the box. Shining, was a silver heart shaped locket.

My eyes widened as I moved my face closer towards it. Gently, the locket floated in front of me on its own. My jaw nearly dropped. *Mom? Was she here?* I looked around the room. I was still the only the person here.

"How is this possible?" My arms broke out into goosebumps. The front of the locket was missing. Its body was decorated with tiny engraved swirls and flowers that sparkled. It was beautiful. Mesmerized like a trance, I slowly reached my hand out towards it.

When the tip of my fingers touched the locket, I saw a flash of a woman draped in a black hooded cape. Her hood covered most of her face, only showing the tip of her nose and pink lips. She laid on a dampened ground in an old, dark stone tunnel, nearly lifeless.

I thought she was dead, until she uttered the words: *"Promise me."*

"Ahhhh!"

I pulled my hand back. It went to my mouth, and my other hand went to my chest, just above my heart. It sped, while the rest of me shook and panted. My heart only started to calm when I realized that I was back in the living room. The locket had fallen to the floor. I breathed in and out to calm my heart and to stop my shaking. My eyes fixated on the locket. I looked at the digital clock on the wall. It was still before midnight. Only a few minutes had passed. I gazed back at the locket.

Was I dreaming? It had to have been a dream. There was no other logical explanation. My imagination must have gotten away with me. However, the fact that someone felt the need to hide a box that only held a necklace and a blanket was odd. I gazed back down at the locket. It continued to sparkle on the floor. I bent down towards it. I hesitated, but ultimately I decided to scoop the locket back up into my hands. It glowed.

My eyes widened.

"Promise me," it whispered.

With a gasp, I pulled my hands away and dropped the locket. I looked around. I was still alone. My mind must have been playing tricks on me. Goosebumps rose along my arms.

"I can't do this. I have to go bed," I whispered.

I grabbed the blanket and wrapped it around the locket. I stuffed them both back into the box and placed them back into the hole. I rose to my feet.

The hole! Darn it, how do I close the hole? Do I stuff it with something? What? No. That would be too obvious. Wait, how did it even get here? It wasn't here before. Let's see, what was everything that happened before the hole appeared? I put the globe back on its stand after hitting the book case too hard, and…Wait.

I ran over to the book case. I looked back at the hole. I looked forward, and then up at the globe. I doubted that the globe had anything to do with it, but just in case— I levitated the globe up from its stand. I turned my head over my shoulder. The hole was still there. I turned my head back and levitated the globe down into its stand.

Huh. That left the bookcase. I placed both hands against the edge of a shelf. Maybe it had to do more with that? I stretched one hand towards the globe again, holding it place. And with both the raw strength of my other hand and telekinesis, I hit the bookcase again, colliding it into the wall.

I looked back over my shoulder. Silver metal plates that matched the rest of floor appeared on all sides inside the square hole. They each moved towards the center, making the hole smaller and smaller, until it disappeared into the floor.

I sighed, converting any worry or stress into relief. Yet, I still pondered the question: *Why are my parents hiding jewelry in the floor?*

And that flash of the woman… Goosebumps on my arm rose, again. *No! Don't think about it. Just go to bed. Go to bed. It doesn't matter. Just go to bed.*

I used my gift to unroll the rug back into its place, and to rearrange all of the furniture as they were before.

"Lights off." I ran into the hallway as the room darkened.

Quietly, I sneaked into the bedroom that Hannah and I shared. I climbed into my bed. Hannah was sound asleep.

I laid my head down on my pillow and pulled the white covers over it. As my eyes closed, and I slowly began to drift off into slumber, I heard a strange whisper in the back of my ear. It was different from the woman's voice in the tunnel. This voice was deep and distinguished in tone. It spoke: *"Finally, I have found you."*

VOICES

Knock-knock-knock!
"Alex, are you up?" Mom was on the other side of the door.
"Yeah," I grumbled, still in bed.
She opened the door and walked in. She pulled the covers from my head and I closed my eyes tighter.
"Sweetheart, it's almost midday." She sat down on the bed next to me.
"I'm just tired," I mumbled.
I wanted to keep my eyes shut, but Mom had other plans. "Come on. Sit up. Up, up, up!"
I sat up like she said, but not without my groans. My eyes peeped opened as I yawned.
"I want to talk to you about yesterday," she said.
I gazed down at the sheets, fiddling my thumbs.
"Alex, look at me," she said, sternly.
I titled my head up towards her.
"Now, I know that you've always had a thirst for the outside. And although you've never met her, I have to say that you are just like your grandmother. She was always considered the odd one in comparison to most of us psychics; always wanting us kids to understand the outdoors instead of being wrapped up inside with our inventions and tech and books as most of us do. So believe me, I really do understand. I even have fond memories as such." She smiled. "But we do not live in that time anymore."
"I know," I muttered.
"Alex."
"I've heard the speech before."
"Then maybe you need to start listening to it!" Her tone was sharp

and I fell silent. "What you did must never happen, again. Do you understand me?"

"Yes, ma'am," I said, softly.

"Good." She leaned in and kissed the top of my forehead. "Now, get up."

She rose to her feet.

"But, I'm still tired!" I protested.

"Good, maybe that means you'll get into less trouble. Now, there is food for you in the kitchen, and in fifteen minutes, your father is going to start your lessons."

"Can't I skip it, just this once?"

"No, now get up."

As I stood up, I asked: "If I'm going to be stuck down here for the rest of my life, do I really need to study?"

"Yes, because I said so. Now stop whining, put on some suitable clothes, and go learn about the country that you live in."

Mom left the room, and I did as instructed. I changed from pajamas and to a plain grey t-shirt and pair of dark slacks. I walked to the mirror.

Eh, I thought.

I had crust at the corner of my eyes, and my hair was a bird's nest. I took a tissue and wiped my eyes. I finger-combed my hair, and then picked up a spare hair band, and used it to tie my hair back into a mid-ponytail, with a mane that touched just below my shoulder blades. As always, the hair at the edges of my forehead fell into long bangs along the sides of my face, but this time frizzy. I looked back at my reflection and mumbled. "Yup. Good enough."

I left the bedroom and walked into the living room to find Hannah sitting on the couch, by herself. And, Dad across from her, sitting in a sofa chair.

"Alex..."

"What?" I asked.

"Oh hey, Bedhead. You finally woke up," Hannah said. She stared at me for a moment and tilted her head. "Are you okay?"

"Yeah, who said my name?"

"What are you talking about?" Hannah asked.

"You must still be dreaming," Dad said. "Grab the bowl of the oatmeal waiting for you on the counter, then come have a seat."

I walked over to the counter. My hands touched the bowl, then I heard the voice again: *"Alex."*

I looked over my shoulder. There was only Hannah and Dad sitting on the couch, speaking with each other.

Maybe I was still dreaming?

"The Age of the Dawning?" Dad asked Hannah.

I turned my attentions back to the bowl. I picked it up and walked towards the couch.

"Eight hundred years ago, at the end of the Black and White War. Lord Stanburg defeated Lord Payne on the Brigmount Battlefield. Lord Payne had twice as many men, but he was not prepared for Lord Stanburg's hidden trenches, filled with huge stakes, which killed both their men and horses alike during the battle. Or the tunnels beneath the grounds, which allowed Lord Stanburg's spies to learn of Lord Payne's tactics and plans before they were even executed," Hannah said.

"Excellent. And the unification?" Dad asked.

Hannah opened her mouth, but before she spoke, I asked, "This again?"

I plopped down into the sofa beside Hannah.

"Alright, Alex then. The unification?" Dad asked.

"Lord Payne died in battle, and Lord Stanburg was crowned king, and he united the noble families and all of the clans of the psychics under his reign, which still stands today," I answered.

"Good. What else?"

"What else? What else is there?"

Neither Dad nor Hannah spoke.

I looked at Dad and then at Hannah.

"Hannah, don't help," Dad said.

I sunk further into the couch.

"What were the other events that led up to his coronation? How was his rule?"

"It was…good?"

"Was it? What happened during it?" Dad asked.

"Good things?"

Damn. My mind was drawing blank.

"The McCallister Prisoner Exchange? The Braxton Uprising? The Silver Nuptial Decree between the telepaths and telekinetics? Neither you nor your sister would be alive today if it weren't for that decree," he said.

"Dad—" I began.

He cut me off. "We are the parallels of history. It's important to learn from the past so we do not repeat their mistakes, especially the past of our own country, when its consequences still impact us today."

I clutched the edges of the bowl.

"Alex, we live in difficult times. When the time comes to leave this place, you have to have as much knowledge as possible. We all do," he said.

Dad cleared his throat. "Hannah, The Ordinance of Rights?"

Later that day, I lied on my bed in my room. I stared at the ceiling. Wondering. Pondering. I thought about my mother's words. She was right about one thing. I had always had a thirst for the outdoors, even when I was small. So much of a thirst that when I was six years old, Hannah and I stole our parents' yellow highlighters, and used the last of them to draw crookedly-shaped stars above our heads. Well, at least mine were crooked. Hannah was good at drawing, even back then.

I had complained for weeks for not being able to see them, even for a second. So Hannah said, "If we cannot go to the stars, then we will bring the stars to us."

Mom was furious, of course. But she concluded that the highlights couldn't be washed off, so they stayed. I snickered in delight. To this day, I question that conclusion.

"Alex," The voice spoke, again.

"What?" I sat up.

"The locket," it said. It appeared behind my ear. I turned my head, but saw that no one was there.

Crash!

"Oh shoot!" Mom's voice echoed from the other side of the door.

I hopped to my feet and went out into the hallway. I found my mother, bent over by the couch, trying to pick up a thick book with a black plastic cover.

She looked up and nearly jumped.

"Oh Alex, you startled me. I didn't know that you were there," she said.

"Oh, I heard something, but I see that it was nothing. I can—"

"No, come sit. I want to show you something."

I walked over to her, and we both sat down beside each other on the couch.

"Your father is training your sister on telepathy in the training room, so it's just you and me, which gives me time to show you a few photographs that I don't think I've shared before. I keep this album in your father's and I's bedroom," Mom said.

She opened the book and revealed two medium-sized, colored photographs on each page. The book revealed images of children, either spread out or huddled together, playing both indoors and outdoors. Instead of underground all of the dwellings were above ground, in tall, square, gray buildings. They stood close together, with barely any space for trees or bushes between them; mostly only enough for green grass. In front of those homes was a rectangular concrete path right before a black-top street.

"Wow." I looked up at my mother, and she was still looking down at the album, completely mesmerized by the pictures. Her eyes fixated on them. Slowly, she grazed her fingertips across the photographs.

"So." I looked down at the photographs, again. "Who are all of the kids?"

"Neighbors, cousins, random kids down the street, you name it."

"That must have been nice."

"It was, and hopefully one day we can all have that again."

"So…" I began, unsure if I should I even ask my question. "What ever happened to all of those kids?"

"Well, we all grew up and went our own separate ways. Most of us lost contact before the war even started. Life goes on."

"That's it?"

"I'm afraid so."

"You don't believe her, do you? That's a very vague explanation," the voice said.

My eyes widened and my chest perked up.

"Alex, is something wrong?" Mom asked.

"Uh no, just thought that I heard something. It was nothing." I leaned my back into the couch and gripped my left arm with my hand. It was nothing. It was just in my head.

Mom flipped the page and revealed a photo of a full-figured woman with a vibrant smile and wavy, deep red velvet locks that reached past her shoulders. She sat in a wooden rocking chair, holding an infant wrapped in a white blanket.

"Who's that?" I asked.

Mom smiled.

"That's my Great Aunt Roselyn, when she was younger. So…" Her fingers went to her chin. "I suppose your Great, Great Aunt Roselyn." She chuckled. "Now, she was a spunky piece of work, and had a death glare that could kill, which kept the entire family in line."

"And, the baby?" I asked.

"Your grandmother."

Mom pointed at other pictures on the page, showing images of her mother as a child. She turned the page and revealed a multitude of redheads, auburn locks, and a few brunettes, all smiling in a group photograph, outdoors by the blacktop street.

"Look." She pointed at another photograph.

A thick, tall man stood with full, wavy, peppered white-and-black hair that hung down to his ears. His face bore a thick mustache, and his eyes were surrounded in long lines as he squinted with a wide smile on his face.

"That's my grandpa, Thomas Berry. Ha-ha, we called him Pop Pop. He's where you got your beautiful black hair from," Mom said.

I reached behind me and gently pulled the tip of the tail of my mane into my frame of vision. I gazed down at it. When I looked up, I was greeted by my mother's smile.

"You always said that this gene was in the family," I said.

She chuckled, again. "Of course it is, Sweetheart. How else would you have inherited it?"

She playfully poked me with her elbow and I grinned. Mom flipped another page. I let go of my hair and turned my attentions back to the album.

There was an older, plumb woman, with gray hair pinned back into a bun, sitting in the same wooden rocking chair, holding a book. She appeared to be reading it to two children. Unfortunately, the picture only showed the back of the two girls' heads. Both had long, wavy locks. One with the color of auburn, and the other of deep red velvet.

"Aunt Roselyn, only much older. She used to read to us." Her voice was calm, but her face beamed with happiness.

"Is this one you?" I asked, pointing to the auburn-haired child.

"Yes," she smiled.

"Who's the other girl?" I asked.

"What?" Mom turned to me, startled.

"The other girl? Is she a cousin or something? She has the same hair as Aunt Roselyn when she was younger."

"Right. Cousin, of course." My mother's tone shifted. She tried to hide her nerves behind a weak smile, and she closed the album. "Maybe that's enough photographs for now."

"Mom?"

"Alex, that's enough for now."

"But I only asked—"

"Alex!" she interrupted. "I said that's enough. That's probably too many memories for one day. Maybe, you should go see your father and Hannah. They should be almost done with her training by now. You should go start your physical training with your father."

She held the album close to her chest. I watched her stand up and walk off into the hallway. She went into her bedroom. Soon after, the sounds of the door closing and the latch of the lock clicking echoed into the corridor.

"That is suspicious. It was only a question."

A couple of days had passed since my mother's odd behavior. It hadn't returned. However, it did bring up the question of my parents' pasts. Yes, I had heard the story of how they met, and a few descriptions of the people of Mom's past besides the album that she recently showed me, yet it was never a full picture. Why be so vague? Dad had always been private. I had always just assumed that was just him being him.

Nonetheless, the more I questioned and thought about their potential pasts', the more a lump grew in the back of my throat. They had the very youth and childhood that they denied me. Looking at those photos with Mom was the closest I'd ever come to understanding an actual place with real people outside of these walls. Not people in books or tales, but real people. A different time. And it ended so abruptly. Why me? Why were my parents allowed such a normative in their childhoods', while I was being denied it for some war that I had never seen?

The lights were bright, and the room was hot. I was surrounded by gray tiles and cinder blocks. Loose strands of my hair were plastered to my forehead, while the rest of my hair was pulled back. The edges of my face were wet with sweat. I panted as my arms were stretched out and my hands held a heavy metallic bow staff, tightly gripped between my fingers. Right. Left. Right. Left. I faced my opponent, the long shadow that stretched from my feet to the wall.

I swirled and spun the staff, never taking my eyes off my opponent. My feet were light and not afraid to move as the shadow mimicked my every move. *"We haven't spoken today."* The voice crept into the back of my ears.

I continued. Right. Left. Right. Left.

"You are very talented, I see."

I spun and flipped the other end of the staff towards the wall, without letting it go. *"It is a shame. Your parents—"*

"Enough about my parents!" I warned.

I spun around, attempting the same move again.

"If they can't tell you the truth, the whole truth, then what else are they hiding from you? The jewelry—"

"It's a stupid piece of jewelry." Right. Left. Right. My feet danced in coordination with the swings of my arms. "What does that have anything to do with anything?"

"Your parents are responsible for that young woman."

"What? What are you taking about?"

"That young woman is dead."

"No!" I stopped. I was taken aback by those words. "That's the most ridiculous thing that I've ever heard. They could never hurt or kill anyone." I dismissed the accusation. My lips even oozed with disgust. Unfair. Over-protective. Too strict. Sure. But they weren't killers.

I rolled my eyes. "Now if you will excuse me—"

"They are lying to you."

"My parents are not liars. And they are not definitely killers. They're just too strict."

"Then, why is it that the moment you start asking too many questions, they come to a strong stop? They have to be hiding something."

"Stop it! You're lying."

"Am I? Your mother suddenly stopped when you asked about the little girl. And I bet that if you tried with your father, he would do the same thing. You are a loyal daughter, despite how they treat you."

"I said, ENOUGH!" I swung in anger. The staff collided into my other forearm.

"AHHH!" I dropped the staff and it clanged against the tiled floor. I fell to my knees. I held my arm with my other hand as it turned red and throbbed.

The door swung open. The emergence of more light filled the room, and cast another shadow against the wall.

"Alex, are you alright?" Mom ran up to me.

"It's fine. I'm fine," I said.

"What happened!?" Mom knelt down next to me. She looked down at my arm. "Did you have an accident with the staff? Your arm is already turning red."

She reached. As her fingertips touched my arm, I saw a quick flash of the tunnel; the stone tunnel from the locket. I jumped with my heart nearly pouncing out of my chest.

"Ahh!" My hand left my arm and went to my heart.

"Alex, what's wrong? Does it hurt that bad?" Mom's voice was laced with concern.

"What?" I glanced up at her. I was safe. I was not in the tunnel. I was in the training room. My heart began to slow down.

"I...I..." I wasn't sure what to say. "No, I um, I mean, yeah. Yes, it just hurts really bad."

"Okay, stay here. Enough training for today. I will go get the first aid kit. Stay here. I will be right back."

Mom stood up and ran out of the room. When she returned, she bandaged my arm. We walked out of the training room, up the stairs, and into the main hallway. "You are a good student, Sweetheart. But you don't have to push yourself so hard. That is another discipline that we have taught you, that it is okay to stop or take a break."

I nodded. "I know."

"Let's rest on the bow staff for a few days, okay?"

"Just another thing that they are taking away from you."

"Stop it!" I whispered.

"What?" Mom asked.

"Uh. Nothing. I didn't say anything. I, um, I just thought that I heard some strange noise."

"You just said that you didn't say anything." She crossed her arms, puzzled.

"Right. Sorry. I just…I just I think that I just need some rest. Is it okay, if I just go back to my room?"

"Okay, go ahead. Maybe you're just working too hard. You are your father's daughter."

Beep-Beep!

The sound gently echoed from the living room with a flashing green light.

"Oh. That must be your father calling. Go lay down. I will check on you a little later." Mom walked off.

I turned and began to walk down the hallway. Hannah walked out into the hall from the bathroom. She greeted me with a smile, before her eyes quickly travelled down to my arm. "Hey, what happened to you?"

"Nothing." I continued walking.

Hannah followed. "Alex, are you alright?"

"Yeah, why?"

"I heard tidbits of your thoughts earlier when I was passing by the door that leads to the training room. Were you arguing with someone or yourself? Because, Mom was in the kitchen, and Dad is out."

I stopped and turned to face Hannah. "You were listening to my thoughts, again!"

"Hey, Alex it's not like that or even that serious. Calm down."

My chest knotted. I could not risk Hannah overhearing anything. Not her. Not anyone. "I told you not to do that! I swear, I can't get any privacy in this damn place!"

Hannah took a step back and raised her hands in front of her with her palms facing me. "Listen, I get that you feel trapped sometimes, but I'm just trying to help you. You don't have to yell at me. You sounded distressed, but—" her tone shifted to annoyance— "if you're going to act like this, then maybe you do need time alone."

I turned from Hannah and began to walk down the hallway towards our bedroom door. "Just stay out of my head!"

"Gladly!"

I opened the door and closed it behind me. I leaned up against the door and gently hit the back of my head against it. What was wrong with me? Was I going crazy, talking to some strange voice in my head? Some voice, which should not even be real, despite it feeling more and more real each day?

"Hannah, what is going on?" Mom's voice emerged from behind the door.

"Nothing," Hannah said.

"Really, nothing? Are you covering for your sister, again?"

"I said, it's nothing. Just dramatic Alex being dramatic Alex."

There was silence, until Mom eventually said, "I don't know what has gotten into that girl, but this is not acceptable."

They are the ones with the problem, not you. Is a little privacy too much to ask for?

Knock-Knock-Knock!

"Mom, I'm okay." I laid in bed, face down into the sheets. I clutched my pillow over my head and ears.

Knock-Knock-Knock!

"Mom..."

"It's not Mom."

I gulped. I pulled the pillow off my head and looked over at the door. It was still closed.

That was Dad's voice, echoing in my thoughts.

Block. Punch. Kick. Block. Punch. Kick. I repeated those words in my head. I couldn't risk Dad reading my thoughts. He would think that I was crazy. Although, part of me felt as if that were true. The space between my eyes was smothered with tension and my head ached with weight.

The door opened.

"Dad—" I began.

He walked in.

"Mom told me what happened. Alex, what is going on with you?" His voice was stern. Dad closed the door behind him and walked up to me.

I sat up straight and faced him. I twiddled my thumbs in my lap and looked down at his brown muddied boots. "I'm sorry. I'll apologize to Mom and Hannah," I said, meekly.

"Your behavior is unacceptable."

"I know," I said, and nodded. "I'm sorry. I was just tired, but I know that's no excuse."

Truthfully, I did not have a problem with apologizing to Mom and Hannah. I shouldn't have spoken to them that way.

"You know better."

"I know." I nodded.

"Now, are you going to tell me what's really going on?"

I hesitated before looking up at him. His face was stoic, yet stern. And he was still dressed like our unwanted neighbors, in his hooded cape with the hood down and burlap pants.

"Dad, I just—" I couldn't form the rest of the words in my mouth. Instead, both my eyes and my mouth closed in a sigh. I think a part of me wanted to tell someone, but how could I? They would all just believe that I was disturbed. None of them would understand. They would just find a way to make the lockdown worse.

Block. Kick. Punch. Just repeat those words.

"Alex."

"I'm sorry." I opened my eyes.

"Fine. We can discuss it later. But whatever you are going through or feeling, that is never an excuse for any type of mal behavior. I don't care what happened. You are responsible for how you act. Do you understand me?"

"Yes, sir."

"Good. Arm?"

I stretched out my bandaged arm. He touched both sides of it with his hand. I flinched. I clenched my jaw and held in my yelp.

"It doesn't feel broken, which is good." He turned my arm.

Although he was gentle, I clenched my jaw, further holding in the pain.

He continued: "I know that it hurts, but I just want to make sure that your arm is going to be okay." Dad examined it further. "It looks like it will be fine. Next time you feel tired or off, put down the staff."

He let go of my arm, and I nodded.

"Whatever it is—" Dad placed his hand on top of my head. I was surprised. He hadn't done that since I was a kid. He changed his face. It was no longer stern. It was calm now.

In a warm tone, he continued: "It will be okay. Things have a habit of feeling worse than what they actually are. Rest your arm."

His hand left my head. I watched him as he walked towards the door.

"Dad?"

He stopped.

"What was your life like before the war? What did you do?"

"Your mother said that she showed you pictures of what life was like before the war."

"Yeah, but that was her childhood. What was your childhood like? Or, what did you and Mom do as adults before the war?"

"I worked in my parents' grocery store from a childhood into adulthood. I met your mother. We got married. We had Hannah. Then, you. Then, the war."

"Okay. Then—" I tried to think of the right words. "What was it like to work in a grocery store and what was that life like? Did you have friends? You've told Hannah and I that Grandpa was the one that taught you how to fight. Who taught him?"

Dad turned back around. "His father and his father before him and so on. You could say that it is a family tradition."

"And the grocery store?"

"A lot of hard work and patience, especially when dealing with people." He smirked with an almost-smile as he looked up, as if he had come across a fond memory. He looked back at me. "I doubt you want to be bored with the on goings of stocking shelves."

I almost smiled, as well.

"People. What was that like? Can you tell me more about what your life was like? I don't care if stocking shelves is boring. Can you tell me more about the store? What having a job was like?" All of the questions slipped from my lips quickly.

Dad's face softened even more. He walked back over to my bed and sat down beside me. "As a boy, every morning I trained with my father. Afterwards, I had school lessons with my mother, and then I worked in our family's store in the evening and on weekends. Most of the time, we only sold produce. However, there was one shelf that sometimes held books that Father—" He looked over at me. "Your grandfather sold on discount what we received from other prominent stores that couldn't sell. And sometimes, if I stocked and bagged groceries fast enough, your grandfather would let me have one of the books. Books on aircrafts were my favorite."

"Was that your only job? The onion boy in the Knight Chronicles had many different jobs. He was a farm hand, shoe shiner, and a delivery boy before he became a squire, and then a knight!"

"Alex, that is just a story. It's not real."

"Okay. Well, what else happened in your life? What was Grandpa like as a trainer? Did you ever have to use it to defend yourself?"

"Anyone can find themselves in a situation where they have to defend themselves. You do not start violence, but you have—"

"…every right to protect yourself," we both said, in unison.

I continued: "I know. I was just curious if you or Mom ever had to defend yourselves a lot with all of the conflict you've said is on the outside. Back then, or when you go out now. Were times really peaceful before and everything just happened all of the sudden?"

"Nothing happens suddenly. It was always brewing. But it was a different time."

"So, what happened? What specifically caused us to go into hiding? You've never come back hurt any time you've gone outside."

"Alex, war is dangerous. You don't need to see it to know that. Your mother and I decided that this was the best option to keep the family safe. You have no idea what panic and paranoia that causes in neighbors, as well as our enemies. We would not have been able to keep you or your sister from harm."

"So, what happened? What did the panic do to them?"

"It was nothing that you have to worry about now."

"Why won't you tell me? You and Mom never go into specifics.

What happened?"

"There doesn't need to be specifics. My job is to keep you all safe. That is all that you need to know."

"Dad. Come on. Anything? You can't tell me anything?"

He put his hand on the top of my head. "Get some rest," he said.

His hand left my head. He stood back up and began to walk back towards the door. I bit my bottom lip. *Maybe, I could ask a different question?*

"Is our family still alive?"

Dad stopped.

"Get some rest, Alex. We can discuss that at a later time."

He continued towards the door. He opened it and walked out, closing it behind him.

"Are you sure that he is not the one who is paranoid?"

THE LOCKET

Sleepless night after sleepless night, I suffered, further haunted by the voice. It continued to whisper into my ear, prodding and picking. It was my predator, and I was its prey. It was never-ending.

It was dark. I was in the cinder tunnel. I wrapped my arms around myself, trying to keep warm from the cold, moist air. My toes curled as water from the ground slowly seeped into my shoes. I closed my eyes, holding myself closer. As the temperature began to drop, my body began to shiver.

When I opened my eyes, the woman, draped in the dark, hooded cape, appeared before me. She had collapsed on the ground. She laid still on her back in a detailed silk gray gown that touched the tip of her brown boots. The gown was damp with traces of mud along its skirt. Her cape covered her shoulders and arms. Her hood hid her eyes, exposing only the tip of her nose and her pink lips. I jumped back against the wall, digging my nails into my arms. My heart raced and my vocal cords froze. Slowly, she began to turn her head towards me. The sound of my beating heart pulsed through my ears. I pressed myself further into the wall, allowing its tiny ridges to pierce into my skin.

"Promise me," she said.

"AHHHH!!!!!" I opened my eyes and woke up in my bed. I sat up, tightly clutching my covers. My whole body trembled and my forehead was wet with sweat. I placed one hand over my heart. It felt heavy, as if there were some type of weight resting on top of it. I looked over at Hannah's bed. It was empty. Her blanket and sheets were neatly tucked and dressed on the bed as if no one had ever slept in it.

I examined the room. Everything looked the same. Everything was in place. The closet doors were shut. The dresser had not been moved.

It was spotless on Hannah's side, with only the framed picture of her and our parents. On my side of the dresser were a couple of books with loose black hair bands and a large hair brush and comb.

I sighed in relief.

My hands went to the sides of my face, and my fingers laced themselves into the edges of my hair. "Only a dream," I whispered.

I took a deep breath, attempting to calm my nerves. "You're okay. I'm okay. Just a dream. Remember, it was only just a dream."

I stepped out of my bed.

Thud!

A noise echoed from the hall. Quickly, I twisted around. My feet stepped over themselves, and I fell onto the floor.

"Alex, are you alright in there?" Mom called.

I looked down at my hands. They refused to stop shaking. I pulled them in close. "You're okay. I'm okay. Just a dream. Remember, it was only just a dream," I whispered, again.

I walked out of the bedroom and into the kitchen. Dad and Hannah were already sitting at the counter eating a bowl of plain oatmeal, while Mom was stirring a small pot over the stove. Hannah looked at me and nearly dropped her spoon.

"Hey, what happened to you? You look as if you've seen a ghost," she said.

I continued towards the counter and said, "Yeah… um…I just…I just couldn't sleep. Bad dream, last night. That's all."

I sat down and avoided eye contact with everyone by simply staring down at the countertop.

"Alex, are you sure that you are okay?" Mom asked.

I nodded yes, though all I could think about was the dream. My thoughts were riddled with flashes of the tunnel and that woman. I shook my head, trying to shake out the images. I looked up to see my family's glances. They were all trying to pretend not to stare, but they were not able to hide it well.

"Here, let me get you a bowl." Mom waved her hand and, with telekinesis, opened one of the cabinet doors above the stove. Before she levitated a bowl into the air, Dad said, "Wait—"

"Hannah," he turned towards her. "Why don't you try materializing an exact replica of one of your mother's bowls in front of Alex?"

"Now?" questioned Hannah.

"Yes."

"I don't think—" she began to say.

"Have you not been studying been the molecular structure, like I've instructed you to?"

"No, I have…"

While they continued to talk, my mind wandered back to the dream, back to the tunnel.

"It is the next step in your training," Dad pressed.

"Okay."

Their voices became fainter. I saw more flashes of the woman, each image faster than the one before.

"Here, let me show you," Dad said.

"Promise me."

"Ah!" I yelped and nearly jumped out of my seat. My heart raced and my forehead began to dampen at my hairline. Both of my parents and sister starred at me.

"Alex," Hannah's voice was soft. She reached out her hand towards mine, but I pulled my hand away and placed it in my lap.

"Sweetie, what's wrong? What's going on?" Mom asked.

"I…um, I thought I was dreaming. Like I said, bad dream," I said. I doubted they were convinced.

I looked down at the counter and saw a bowl sitting in front of me.

"What is this?" Cautiously, I leaned further back into the chair. "This wasn't here before!"

"Alex, that's a bowl. Dad just materialized it. Remember? We were just talking about that, " Hannah said, cautiously.

"Oh, yeah." I nodded.

Mom walked up to me and placed her hand on my forehead. "You don't feel warm."

"No, I think it's just sleep. Can I be excused?"

Mom leaned forward, and whispered, "Sweetie, are you sure that nothing is going on? You've been claiming to be tired a lot, lately. If something is going on you can tell me."

I shook my head, 'no.'

"Bad dreams," I said.

Mom stood up straight. She sighed. "Eat something first, even if it's just a little."

She levitated the pot of oatmeal to the bowl and poured the oatmeal into the dish. "There you are. Oh wait, I almost forgot a spoon," she said.

"No need, Gabby." Dad extended his arm with his palm faced down toward the countertop and, in a matter of seconds, he materialized a small silver spoon.

I took the spoon and began eating the oatmeal in small bites. Mom walked away and sat in a chair across from me. We all ate in silence. The voice transferred from the woman's whisper back to the more distinguished voice that originally plagued my mind. Only now it kept whispering, *"The locket…"*

After breakfast, I retired back to my bedroom.

"The locket."

"Please, go away. I just want this to stop," I whispered.

I walked up to the dresser and stared at my reflection in the mirror. My hair was unkempt, with strands coming out of its ponytail. My eyes were outlined with darkened circles underneath them, and my face was pale. Of course, they knew something was wrong with me. Something *was* wrong with me.

"The locket."

"Shut up!" I bent my head down and laced my fingers through my hair, digging my nails into my scalp. "Just. Leave. Me. Alone!"

"Take the locket."

"NO!" I looked up at my reflection in the mirror. I let go of my scalp, though my fingers were still entangled in my hair. My pupils widened at my image in the mirror. My voice turned somber as I asked: "Why would I want something that has clearly started this whole thing?"

"The dreams are only warnings. Your parents are lying to you. They are not the people that you were raised to believe they are. I am your friend."

"A friend?" I allowed my hands to fall to the dresser. "What type of friend would do this? Haunt someone as much as you have haunted me? Or rather haunt someone at all?"

"A friend that understands the severity of the situation. Think of the childhood that your parents had, which they continue to deny you. Do you

think that is fair or right? The locket will show you the truth, and I want you to know the truth."

"But..."

"Hey!"

I jumped. I turned around and saw Hannah standing in the doorway.

"I thought you said that you were tired?" she asked.

"Yeah. I, um, I just thought that I saw something is all."

"Alex, what's wrong?" Her voice was calm, weaved with concern.

I turned away from her. I still couldn't bring myself to tell her the truth. She would think that I was even crazier than I currently looked. She would never understand me hearing voices inside my head. If she told Mom and Dad, they would just become stricter. My fingertips traveled up to my mouth, and my nails gently pushed against my teeth.

"Nothing. It's like I said at breakfast, I've just been having trouble sleeping lately."

"Bullshit." Hannah crossed her arms, "You don't get nightmares. Do you want to tell me what's really going on?"

"You read my thoughts again?"

"No. I didn't have to. I could hear you mumbling something outside the door."

"Well, it doesn't matter."

"Alex, talk to me." Hannah almost sounded desperate. She closed the door behind her and faced me. "Okay, what is going on?"

Block. Punch. Kick. Block. Punch. Kick. Just repeat those words. Don't let her read your thoughts.

"Come on, it's me. You've been acting weird for weeks, even for you. Are you really taking the lack of being outside this hard?"

"It's complicated. It's just—" The worst part is that a part of me wanted to tell her. "It's nothing."

I turned away and walked over to my bed. Hannah sighed behind me. As I sat on my bed, she went over to her bed. She bent down and pulled out a small cardboard box from underneath the bed. She opened the lid, pulled something out and into her hand, and shoved the box with the lid on top back underneath her bed.

Sitting on the edge of the bed, like me, she held out a hair band with a rose gold, rose pin attached to it. "Did I ever tell you why this was always so important to me?" she asked.

"Not really, but you were always more into that stuff than I ever was." Hannah grinned.

Her palm laid flat with the hair band in the center of it. She gazed down with eyes seemingly mesmerized by the pin.

"You probably don't remember; but one time when you were about one and a half, maybe two and I was about four or so, something happened. Ha-ha. The alarms went off. The whole living room flashed red, and I just remember Mom and Dad freaking out and hurrying us all into the escape the room. Dad held you and I clung to Mom."

She faced me and continued: "In hindsight, I don't know if it really was a real threat or not and back then, I'm sure that I didn't understand what was really happening, only that it was something bad."

Hannah looked back down at the hair band. "But Mom smiled at me. She hugged me tight, and gave me this. She told me that as long as I had it, I would be safe. And sure enough, after a while the alarms stopped, and we were all safe again. And ever since, I've always kept this in a safe place, just in case of an emergency. Where I could quickly grab it, and then everything would be okay. Now, I know that it's probably hard to believe that this little thing really could have protected us, but so far so good, right? So, I want you to have it."

"What? Hannah you really don't have to. You know that—"

"Yeah, I got the hint the first time. You're the first and only girl I've ever met not to be into jewelry."

"I'm the only girl that you've ever met," I scoffed.

"Exactly. Which automatically makes you the first."

Hannah scooted behind me on the bed and gently grabbed my hair.

"Now hold still." She let my ponytail down and combed my hair with her fingers. She pulled it back up and into a ponytail with her hair band. "Hopefully this helps."

Hannah hugged me, and then scooted off the bed.

"When you're ready to tell me, tell me. 'Kay," she said.

"Kay," I answered.

Hannah turned towards the door and walked out of the room.

I turned my head towards the mirror and just stared at my reflection.

That night, I laid awake in bed. I was hugged tightly by a warm thick blanket, soft purple pajamas that pressed against my skin, and cozy white socks that soothed my feet. The light sounds of Hannah snoring travelled to my ears, while my eyes travelled up to the poorly drawn yellow stars that stretched across the ceiling. Well, at least the stars that I had drawn. I bit my bottom lip, trying not to smile. They reminded me of Hannah's optimism and her belief of attempting to see the good in everything. I never shared this exact belief, though I would be lying if I said that weren't days in which I needed it. I rolled over onto my side and closed my eyes.

I laid still for a few minutes, until I heard the whisper. *"The locket."*

I ignored it.

"The locket."

"Enough about this damn locket! Will you shut up and leave me alone!?" I whispered. I covered my ears with my hands, as if that could help.

"I am only trying to help you."

I scoffed. "And why should I trust the voice that has been constantly torturing me?"

"Have I lied to you once?"

"My parents aren't killers. I don't know how many times I have to say that. What ever happened to that woman, my parents had nothing to do with it."

"Then prove me wrong. Let the locket show you the truth. Or if you insist, then do continue to live out this lie."

"It's not a lie."

"Is it not? You already know that your parents are paranoid. If that is the case, then how do you know if this war is even real? They want to keep you trapped. You've never even seen it, and you've even said yourself, your father has never come back hurt from the outside."

"Well, my parents are paranoid. But they're—" I hesitated. I almost could not form the rest of words in my mouth. I closed my eyes and tightly clutched my sheets in my hands. I didn't even believe the words that I was about to say. "They're just trying to protect us."

"Is that what you think? Or what Hannah thinks?"

I opened my eyes.

What did I think?

"You're different than Hannah. You think for yourself. You know that your parents aren't telling you everything. That is obvious."

"No one tells anyone everything. Even the characters in my books don't."

"Yes. And, what happened to those characters?"

"They—" I began, but the words did not continue.

"Like I said, prove me wrong, friend. Or not. The choice is yours."

I sat up, letting go of my ears. I glanced over at the door. The air lightly buzzed with Hannah's snoring. Carefully, I stepped out of bed and sneaked out from my room into the corridor and into the living room. Just as before, I used my gift to push the furniture back. I walked over took the bookshelf. I held the globe still in its stand on top of the book shelf with telekinesis, and shook the bookshelf against the wall. I made the edges of the rug roll itself up, and push itself back into the bottom of the couch. The compartment in the floor opened. I walked over to it, and inside lied the wooden box. I opened the box and levitated the locket into the air.

"Take it."

I pulled it towards me, and slowly reached out my hand out to touch it.

"Richard."

I ducked down at the sound of my mother's voice, and the locket fell to the floor.

"Are you sure about this?" she continued.

I crawled behind the couch. Their bedroom door cracked open, and the light from their room shone onto the wall. Neither of them came into the hallway. Instead, only their shadows were present.

"Positive. If any of those wics—" Dad began.

"Language," Mom interrupted. "You know that I don't like that type of language in this house."

"Sorry, Gabby. I just get worked up."

"Fine." Mom folded her arms. "But how do we know that this will actually work?"

"I've been working on it for months, and now that it's finally done, it should be able to solve the problem that we've been having with Alex," Dad said.

Mom mumbled. I couldn't make out her words.

"I know," Dad said.

"And if it…?"

"It won't. It will enhance the overall system and make it nearly impossible for anyone to escape. It will further our protection from the outside, too. You are right about not knowing when the war will eventually be over. This should ease any worry about that, until it finally does end."

"You see; you don't even need the locket to show you what your family will do."

"It doesn't matter. There isn't a system that I can't beat," I said.

"Are you sure? They want to keep you here, trapped with them in their own delusions. This war is fictional. Have you ever even seen a soldier? A battle? Or anything?"

"I'm just a little uneasy about testing it out," Mom said.

"Only you and I will have the code and this new system will alert all of the monitors if anyone from the inside does try or attempt any kind of escape. No backdoor. I made sure of that," Dad said.

My chest tightened.

How could he do this? How am I supposed to get to the outside? It was bad enough that I had to space out my escape attempts months at a time. Now, this?

"Like I said, have I ever lied to you? You must run. Run before it's too late, far away from here."

The voice was right, but I couldn't just run away. Despite my feelings of being trapped, this was my home. My only home.

"Alright. I'm just a little worried—" Mom began.

"Don't be. Watch. It will only take three minutes to activate."

The clutch of the latch clicked as my parents tightly closed their bedroom door.

"But if you really wish to stay, then you should stay. Maybe cherish one last moment outside? Remember, I'm your friend and I only want to help. What's one last outing?"

"Just one last one," I whispered. Now, that didn't seem so bad. I could savor it before being doomed down here forever. My parents would never know. What would be the harm? The new system was for escaping, not sneaking back inside. Dad would never get rid of the retina scan. That wouldn't be smart. I would just have to come back before anyone noticed.

"*Three minutes until your father activates the new security system.*"

Quickly yet quietly, I darted to my bedroom. I walked over to my bed, stuffing my pillows underneath the covers, but leaving one at the head. I went over to the closet. I looked back at Hannah. She was now loudly snoring in her bed. "I'll be right back, Hannah," I whispered.

I opened the closest door. I grabbed a brown jacket, tossed it over my pajamas, and quickly ran out into the hallway.

"*One minute.*"

I slipped into a pair of brown shoes and ran into the escape room.

"*Thirty seconds.*"

I typed in the escape code. A large tube fell that encased my body.

"*Twenty seconds.*"

Air appeared into the tube and sucked me up to a hidden door that lied beneath a large bush above ground. It spit me out. I landed on my feet, almost tipping over.

The sun was just now beginning to rise. The sky was still mostly dark with layers of pink starting to awaken. I knew that I had at least an hour, maybe two hours before Hannah and my parents would try to wake me. I had to make this one count.

My last outing…

THE BOY WITH EMERALD EYES

I walked until I reached an old thick oak tree. It was the same spot in which Hannah had found me the last time I snuck out. There was still a little time before I had to head back, so I sat down against the trunk of the tree. I gazed up and my face relaxed into a smile, as I watched the birds and squirrels flutter and scurry along the branches.

I closed my eyes and leaned further back into the tree. I took a deep breath, allowing my nostrils to be filled with the scent of the morning dew and pine cones.

"Get up!"

"Why?" I asked.

Snap!

My ears perked up. It was the sound of twigs breaking. No need to worry, it could have easily been a rabbit or one of the squirrels that I had just seen. I listened for more; however, I soon realized that the chatter and noises of the forest were dying down.

I opened my eyes and stood up with my back still pressed up against the tree. It was now quiet, disturbingly quiet.

"Stay."

I examined my surroundings. I did not see a soul.

The ground beneath my feet began to rumble. It vibrated through my boots. The dirt in front of me rose up in the form a tidal wave and swirled itself around me. I extended my arms and held out my hands on either side of me to push the dirt back. I could feel its walls in my palms as if I were actually touching it. It began to close in, but I pushed harder. What was happening? This had never happened before. The space between the dirt and I grew smaller.

I screamed, letting out more bursts of energy.

I was able to stall it for a few more seconds, but eventually closed around me and encased all my limbs from my chest and down. The soil hardened like stone, and remained stagnate. I wiggled, and my eyes darted back and forth across the trees and bushes.

Snap!

My breath halted. My heart raced through my ear drums and pounded the ribs that encased it.

"Ha-ha." A foreign snicker.

Stepping forth from behind a tree was a husky man with a round face, accompanied by patches of black scruff along his neck and jawline. He wore a brown burlap hat that covered his eyes. On top of his soiled clothes, hung a long, unbuttoned brown jacket that reached his calves.

The beat of my heart echoed louder and louder into my ears with each step towards me that he took. I wiggled faster and harder, but I could not break free. He smirked, seemingly delighted by my fear.

"Now, what's a pretty creature like ye doing out here?" His voice was raspy, yet carried a strange accent. Despite rasp, he spoke with a sort of smoothness, and emphasized each vowel more than other the letters in his words. "Eh?"

He stopped when he was only about six inches from my face. The stranger smiled revealing his yellow stained teeth. I did not respond to his question. Instead, I repeated the words *stay calm* inside my head.

"Ye're not from around 'ere, are ye?"

I nearly gagged at the scent of vomit in his breath.

"Ye even look like a damn syche? *Atema!*"

The dirt encasing me fell to the ground. However, before I fell, the man grabbed my wrist with his fat fingers. He held me up.

My eyes widened. I suddenly realized...he said a word, and then the dirt fell. I was in the hands of a sorcerer. I tightened my body to prevent myself from trembling.

The sorcerer continued: "Now, imagine the heavy amount of gold that I could get for yer head."

Stay calm. I placed my other wrist behind my back and I quickly began to transfer energy into that hand.

He continued, "How about we take a little walk?"

I moved my hand from behind my back to my front at his chest. I focused all my energy and released it in a burst that violently pushed him back, launching him back into a tree.

"How about we not." I stood up, straight.

The sorcerer jumped back onto his feet.

"Ye, filthy little syche!" he yelled.

He lifted up his hand into the air and said, *"Detra Arma!"*

Immediately, I turned and ran. I levitated the dirt, rocks, leaves, twigs, and whatever else I could find up into the air, making them all swirl around as a shield. The sorcerer followed me, shooting blasts of blue lights at me. I ran in zig-zags, jumping over logs and zooming through bushes.

Crap, why did I leave home? I couldn't lead him to Mom, Dad, or Hannah. Or maybe I should? They could help me. No, our home was a secret, and even I couldn't break that secret. What if he gets away and does tell someone, other sorcerers?

"No!" I shrieked at the thought.

I looked back over my shoulder, and to my surprise, the sorcerer had seemingly disappeared. I stopped. My eyes searched, but they couldn't find him. Although the shield was protecting me, it was also hindering my ability to see well beyond it. In a quick decision, I halted it. All of its elements fell to the ground.

"Above you!"

I looked up. The sorcerer was in the air. He was slowly falling down towards me, while forming another magical blast in his hands. Before I could react, I felt myself being pushed to the ground by some force, shoving me out of harm's way. I hit the ground hard and let out a small grunt of pain. My palms stung from where I tried to brace my fall and my heart was still beating uncontrollably.

"Aspedia!"

I looked back and saw the back of someone's head, a new person. A boy? The person was shaped like a boy. He had thick and black wavy hair down to the top of his neck, and similar clothes to the sorcerer that was chasing me, except no jacket or hat. The person held out both of his hands towards the sky. I looked further, following the angle in which they reached.

They led me to the sight of the sorcerer, slowly falling from the sky. Both of his palms were out, and they held a light blue ball of light. The sorcerer released this light from his hands, and then continuously released more blasts. They swirled around us, about to collide into us all at once. I knew that there was no way I would be able to shield myself from such an embrace.

I closed my eyes and clenched the dirt on the ground, dragging its specks underneath my short fingernails. For once, I should have listened to my parents and definitely not to some crazy voice in my head. Now, I'm going to…wait, nothing happened. Instead, I only heard the faint sounds of drums. I opened my eyes, and saw that all of the blasts were being reflected by some transparent light-green dome that surrounded the boy and I. The dome vibrated, but remained steady.

On the outside, there was a large display of different hues of blue, ranging from light to dark as they struck the dome and bounced off. Once reflected, the lights either collided into each other or into the nearby trees, bushes, and other surrounding plants, leaving them with blackened scars. When they struck each other, they both disintegrated into sparkling dust that fell to the ground. It was the most captivating and beautiful sight that I had ever seen in my entire life, yet also the most terrifying.

The area was filled with smoked. Once it cleared, the sorcerer stood only a few feet away. As I stood back up, I looked over at the sorcerer, and then at this new mysterious person.

For moments there was only silence. There was no chatter amongst the forests, nor from amongst any of us; only unnerving quietness. Eventually, the mysterious newcomer turned and looked back at me. His bright emerald eyes complimented his deep olive skin.

Wow. I had never seen eyes of such color before. They were striking. Dad and Hannah had brown eyes, and Mom had hazel eyes. Even in all of the family photographs, everyone's eyes were some hue or shade of brown.

I examined him further. We actually looked around the same age. Perhaps, maybe he was little bit older? I couldn't pinpoint his exact height. I could tell that he was a few inches shorter than the other sorcerer, but definitely taller than me.

Who was he? And what did he want? Why was he even here? Why were either of them here? No one ever came into these woods except for today.

"It's my property, boy!" the sorcerer said.

What? How dare he! I'm a person, not an it! And I sure as Hell am not anyone's property. I balled my fists and glared at him, but he just grinned in the direction of the boy, which made me angrier.

The boy glared back at the sorcerer. "I beg to differ. She's mine."

My jaw nearly dropped, and my heart paused. Before I could react, the newcomer extended his hand towards me and said, *"Capara girl!"*

I felt a strong invisible hold grab my wrist. I gazed down and tried to touch it, but there was no object there to grasp. It felt tight like a fastened rope. The boy motioned his hand towards himself, and this invisible rope quickly shot me towards him.

"Whoa!" I yelped.

My wrist landed right into the grip of the boy's hand.

He leaned into my ear and whispered, "I'm not going to hurt you, just play along."

He turned his attentions back to the sorcerer. "That's right! She belongs to me. Normally, she is much more behaved than this, but she must have run off when I was busy. So, I apologize for any damage or trouble that she may have caused."

"Wha—" I began to ask.

"Sylenko!" He interrupted, waving his hand.

My voice. It was gone. I touched my throat with my other hand, desperately trying to make a noise, but nothing came out. What did he just do to me? I had to get out of here. I attempted to twist out of his grip, but he must have caught on. He twisted my wrist, not enough to hurt, but enough that if I moved, it would.

"It's a feisty one, eh?" asked the sorcerer.

"Aren't they all? So, if that's all settled, then we'll be on our way." The boy turned to leave.

"Hold it, boy," the sorcerer said.

The boy stopped.

"Ye really expect me to believe that this syche belongs to ye?"

Again, I belong to no one!

"That is what I just said," the boy said.

"Hmm?" The sorcerer pondered. "Then, tell me, eh. Why I shouldn't report ye? We all knows the law."

The boy turned back around, facing the sorcerer. He reached into his pocket and pulled out a golden badge with a capital "Z" engraved across it.

The sorcerer hesitated. His eyes widened and his face was laced with surprised. My forehead creased as I examined the strange badge. Was it some type of weird or special object? What power did it hold? What if it was as powerful as a genie or a genie's lamp? Oh, no! If it was, what was going to happen to me?

The sorcerer stood quietly, until he finally asked, "And, His Majesty is aware that on' of his own, especially as young as ye are owns a syche?"

His Majesty? Wait, the king? The king of the sorcerers?

"His Majesty has other and more important matters to attend to than to concern himself with what I do in my free time. Now, unless you want me to find something, which I am most definitely sure there is something that I can and will find to report about you, I suggest you let us on our way," the boy warned.

The sorcerer folded his arms. He tipped his hat further back and laid his gaze upon me. He had sharp, crystal blue eyes and wrinkles that laid both underneath and to the side of them. His mouth smirked into a devilish grin, exposing bits of his yellow teeth.

"Well, I'm sure we can work something out." He looked back at the boy.

"Eh-em," he gnarled his throat. He stood up taller with a clearer voice as if to sound more sophisticated. "Both of our secrets are heavy burdens to keep and I will gladly keep my mouth shut if ye can help ease my burden."

The boy reached into his pants' pocket and pulled out a few bronze coins. He tossed them to the sorcerer's hand.

The sorcerer caught them.

He smirked. "Is this all yer burden is worth to ye? Because it barely eases mine."

The boy's face rested into a glare as he pulled out a small sack of coins. He threw the bag to the sorcerer, who caught it perfectly in the open palm of his hand.

He tipped his hat forward and said, "Pleasure doing business with ye."

"Transmedo!" the boy said.

He and I both vanished.

Meanwhile…

HANNAH

SHE'S GONE

Hannah woke up with a gasp. She sat up in her bed with her hand over her chest, panting. She clutched it, just above her stomach. Her arms were riddled with goosebumps. "Just a dream…only a dream," she said.

She took a deep breath.

The room was still dark. Hannah gazed over at my bed and saw the imprint of the pillows that laid underneath the sheets.

"Alex," she said, softly.

No response.

"Alex, come on. Are you awake?" she asked.

She stared at my covers and hopped to her feet. "Alex," she said again, pulling the sheets back.

She shook her head 'no' while stepping back.

"Not again!"

She darted to the living room, her eyes moving from the couch to the shelves, past the counter and into the kitchen. She ran to the entrance door. There was a petite keyboard by the handle of the door. She typed the code.

"Error! Error! Error!'" read all of the screened monitors in large red letters.

Hannah jumped back. "What the—" she asked.

A small buzzer sounded, and grew louder with each passing second. Hannah hit "cancel" on the keyboard, and then both the buzzer and red alerts stopped.

"What is happening? What did I do?" She pressed her fingernails into the sides of her head. "I have to—"

She ran to our parents' bedroom door and balled her hand into a fist. She nearly touched it. Instead, she stopped.

"Maybe not yet," Hannah whispered.

She opened the palm of her hand and placed it against the door. She closed her eyes and concentrated. She knew enough not to search Dad's mind, but if Dad had changed the system or created a new password, Mom would be the first to know.

"Got it!"

Hannah ran back to the door and typed in the new code. The door opened and she proceeded up the stairs.

Outside, she was met with silence. She closed her eyes. Goosebumps stretched along her limbs and feet, again. This time, they were not due to a bad dream. They were now due to the chilly air and ground. Her face turned worrisome. *Nothing*. She opened her eyes and ran bare foot through the wet morning dew to the same spot that she had found me before.

There, she only found the scent of burning wood, and a path of charred scars on tree trunks that stretched out into the distance.

Snap!

Hannah jumped behind a tree trunk. She turned her head, slightly and cautiously peering out from the tree. She only saw the scarred forestry. She leaned back against the trunk and closed her eyes, once again. As she tightened them, her hands clutched the bark of the trunk.

She groaned, breaking her concentration. Hannah tilted her head forward and down until it met with the touch of her hand. She stared at the ground. She tightened her free hand into a fist and looked up. "Nothing!" she said.

Still nothing.

There were only trees.

Alex, where did you go?

Hannah took another deep breath, and then ran back to the bunker.

"MOM! DAD!" Hannah ran down the metal stairs and into the living room. The door closed behind her.

"Mom!" she shouted, again.

Our parents ran out from their bedroom in their house coats.

"Hannah, what's wrong!? Why are you up so early and…Wait, are you coming from outside!? How were you able to get out there? Where is your sister!? Is she...!?" Mom asked frantically.

Hannah opened her mouth, but her lips did not move. Instead, her thoughts spoke the words: "She's gone."

Dad's eyes widened. His body froze.

"Alex." He spoke softly, barely forming the word in his mouth.

"Wait, what is going on?" Mom asked.

Dad looked over at her. She fell silent, shaking her head and backing away. Her eyes glistened with tears. Quickly, she ran past Hannah. The keys on the keyboard entered the code themselves, and the door re-opened. Mom ran up the stairs.

"I'm so sorry, Dad. I knew something was wrong, but I didn't think that she would actually run off again," Hannah said.

"It's alright." Dad pulled Hannah in for a hug. "Don't worry we'll find her."

Mom ran back down the stairs and said, "I can't sense her."

She spoke as if she could barely breathe. Mom clutched her fingers like claws and began to shake. Tears surfaced in her eyes. "Not her energy or anything. But others...I can sense the presence of others in the forest."

Dad's face turned stern.

"Psychic or sorcerer?" he asked.

"I...I..." Mom began. A few of the tears fell down her cheek.

"Gabby, it's okay." Dad left Hannah and walked over to Mom. He touched her shoulders. "Just think. You have to remember your training. Take a deep breath."

His voice was calm. Mom closed her eyes. She deeply inhaled and exhaled the air out through her nose.

"Remember your training," he repeated.

"Training? The training that you learned from your parents? Dad?"

"Hannah, hush," he said.

"It was...it was um... sorcerer...sorry, it has been so long." Mom trailed off, deep in concentration. "It was... sorcerer...I'm sure of it. Sorcerer."

"Shit!" Dad said.

Mom opened her eyes.

"We have to go." Dad broke away from her and began to walk towards their bedroom.

"Dad, what's going on?" Hannah asked.

"Hannah, stay here," he said as he walked past her.

She turned to Mom.

"It's alright, sweetie. Just do as you are told." Mom's voice changed, as if she had drained most of the emotion from it. She wiped her tears with the back of her hand, and shook herself back into a calmer demeanor, almost stoic.

"What?" Hannah asked, softly. She shook her head and ran after them. "Something is off. What are you not telling me!?"

Hannah entered into their bedroom.

Their room held a full-sized bed with a dark quilted blanket and with gray sheets against a silver metal frame. To the sides were their respective dressers, and directly facing the foot of their bed was their walk-in closet. The walls were mostly bare, except for the line of charcoal childhood sketches of Hannah and I.

Dad walked over to the foot of the bed, while Mom headed straight toward the closest. Dad unscrewed the left corner of the bed post, revealing a series of black buttons. He pushed one of them, and a hidden medium-sized compartment in the floor opened. Inside were a series of weapons: Bow staffs, silver segmented whips, sharpened knives that all varied in blade size from small to large, petite black square tasers, and more.

"What is this?" Hannah asked.

"You've seen weapons like these before," Dad said as he searched through the weapons and took out the ones that he wanted.

"Yes, in the training room. Not hidden beneath the floor! What is going on? Why are you both acting so weird?" Hannah asked.

"Your sister is in danger." Mom was scurrying through the clothes in the closet. She picked up two black holsters from a shelf that was placed above their hanged clothes. She placed one around her waist and threw the other to Dad, who was still bent down beside the open compartment. Mom went back to rummaging through the closest.

"Yes. I know, which is why I don't understand why we're not running out to go find her now! Do you even need all of those! WE'RE WASTING TIME!" Hannah said.

"We will, but you need to calm down and stay here," Dad said.

"Calm down? She's my sister! Mom literally just said that there are—"

"Hannah, you don't understand the gravity of the situation," Dad interrupted.

"Don't understand? I'm the only one freaking out right now! I don't understand why either of you are so calm!"

"Here." Dad extended his hand out towards her, holding a short, thick metal cylinder. His hand squeezed its center, and the device extended itself into a long metal staff.

"Dad?" Hannah was caught off guard. She pondered: *Instead of answering my questions, you want to me to take a weapon?*

"Despite its exterior, it's a lot lighter and stronger than what you're used to. There are two buttons on either side; one to extend and collapse it, and the other releases sharp blades on both ends. Keep it with you at all times until we get back. We are also leaving a few more weapons here just in case."

Hannah walked up to Dad and took the bow staff.

"The escape code? The new one?" he asked.

"What?" Hannah.

"Recite the new escape code. I know that you know it if you were able to go outside."

"52691."

"Good."

Hannah watched as her parents suited their belts up with weapons, our mother levitating them into her pockets and our father strapping them to him by hand.

She looked down at the staff in her hands. "Is this all for the protection from the war, or is there really something else that's also going on?"

"Hannah," Mom began.

"No! You've clearly been hiding something this whole time, and even now you're not telling me anything." Hannah looked over at Dad. "I can sense the blocks that you're putting up on you and Mom's minds."

"Hannah, now is not the time," Dad said.

"Tell me what is going on, now!"

"Sweetheart, I'm sorry, but we can't," Mom said.

"Fine! I'll find go Alex myself." Hannah turned to run, but Mom's telekinesis was too fast. All of her limbs froze in their movements, including her feet, toes, arms, hands, and fingers.

"Let me go, Mom."

"Sweetheart, we don't have time to explain. All you need to know is that we're going to find her and bring her back, safely. But you do need to stay here," Mom said.

"Someone has to be here on the chance that she comes back on her own," Dad said.

"But—" Hannah began to protest.

"No buts. Do you want to make sure that Alex comes back safe and unharmed?" Dad asked.

"Of course, I do," Hannah said.

"Then you will do as you're told," he said.

When Mom finished, she walked up to Hannah, who was still frozen in movement. She hugged her and kissed her forehead. "We will be back. I promise."

"With Alex?" Hannah asked.

Mom nodded. "Yes."

She placed a slender, hard plastic bracelet around Hannah's wrist. "It's a communicator. Press the small button on the side and then speak into the top of the bracelet and you will be able to communicate with us."

Dad walked up to both of them. He placed a wider version of the communicator around his wrist. He opened the top and began typing something in it. The bracelet beeped for a few moments, then stopped.

"What's that?" Hannah asked.

"Activate," Dad said into communicator.

"Tracker global positioning system activated," said the communicator.

"Dad, what is that?"

"Same as yours except with a tracker. It's how we're going to find your sister."

"You have us tracked!?"

"No, only her." Dad took a last glance around the room. His eyes landed on Mom. "Are you ready?"

She nodded.

"It looks like she's already wandered into sorcerer territory," Dad said.

Both Dad and Mom pressed a button that resided on their holsters, and their house coats were digitally transformed into brown hooded capes and traditional sorcerer clothing. Dad wore a long-sleeved white shirt with a brown burlap vest over with brown pants. Mom wore a simple brown dress. The sleeves went down to her wrist, and the skirt of the dress went to her ankles. The items that stayed the same were their holsters and the weapons that resided in them and in their pockets.

Mom turned to Hannah. "Be safe," she whispered.

"And one more thing." Dad placed his hand on Hannah's forehead. "There are a few weapons in there that you are not trained on. Now, you have all of the instructions for them just in case, but still keep the staff by your side at all times."

He removed his hand. Both he and Mom turned towards the staircase.

"But nothing will happen, right?" Hannah asked.

They both stopped.

"Everything is going to be okay, right? You'll find her, or she'll come back on her own, and we'll all be safe again?" Hannah's gaze was wide-eyed, and her voice most desperate for a *yes*.

"Be safe, Hannah. We'll be back soon enough," Dad said.

He and Mom walked up to the stairs and disappeared. Behind them fell the normal door, and then a larger steel door in front of it. A type of door that was rarely used, unless my parents deemed it as an emergency.

The hold on Hannah's body had released itself. Although she could now move, she remained both still and silent as she stared at the metal door.

ALEXANDRIA

KIDNAPPER

I felt as if my entire body had been sucked into a small space as fast as lightning. It was accompanied by a spectrum of the colors of green, brown, blue, purple, and yellow. They all blended together around me. I was involuntarily pulled in only to be spit out a few seconds later. My head spun, and my stomach churned.

My feet touched the ground, but I still felt the force pull me forward. I nearly lost my footing. I stretched my arms and hands out in front of me, and used my gift to keep myself from falling forward.

The boy had also reappeared at my side. He landed swiftly and steadily onto his feet.

"Whoa there, are you okay?" he asked.

He reached his hand out towards my shoulder. I looked from the corner of my eye, and quickly turned to elbow him in the chest. As he gasped, I ran.

"Wait!" he called out.

I ignored him.

I ran straight ahead as fast as I could, until I collided into another invisible wall and fell backwards onto the ground. My head pounded. I looked up, and my eyes were blinded by the sun.

The boy teleported himself beside me. I pushed myself backwards with my hands and feet. He knelt down and said, "That had to hurt."

He extended his hand towards me, but I swatted him away.

"It's okay. It's okay. I'm not going to hurt you."

Yeah, right. I took his hand, and with my other hand, I punched him in the eye.

"Ughhh!"

As his hands went to his face, I took off running again. I held my forehead with one hand, and with the other, I levitated the dirt, leaves, and pebbles around me in the air, and then shot them in all directions. Once they reached approximately thirty feet in all directions, they hit more invisible walls, and fell back to the ground. I stopped running and finally started to look around.

I was still surrounded by forest, but the trees were different. They were shaped differently. Some stretched taller, others shorter or thicker, than the ones near home. The leaves of the bushes held different patterns. There was no chatter of birds or squirrels. And, the air bore a strange scent. It was an intriguing concoction of iron, grass, and acorns. My eyes darted back and forth, and the tips of my fingernails went to my mouth. *How am I supposed to get out of this?* I was trapped. I had no idea where I was, or how close or far away from home. My teeth made quick and tiny bites on my nails as I tried to ponder some way to escape.

Something cold slithered around my ankle. I opened my mouth in surprise, but no sound came out. I jerked my foot forward. Looking down, I noticed a small petite silver charm connected a tiny, slender chain that stretched across the ground.

What?

I reached down to rip it off me, but before I could touch the charm, the chain yanked me to the ground. I hit the dirt hard, with the shock of the impact of seizing my breath.

Dammit!

The boy walked up to me, holding his eye. "WHAT THE HELL IS WRONG WITH YOU!? I think you fuckin' gave me a black eye!"

The skin around his eye was clearly red and starting to bruise.

Good. Let me go, or I will be sure to give you another one!

"Well, aren't you going to say something!?" he asked.

I glared at him, both angry and annoyed.

"Oh, shit! Sorry. I completely forgot." The boy held out his palm. *"Le Magna!"*

I coughed and my hands went to my throat.

"I can speak," I said.

"Yeah, your voice might sound a little raspy for a few minutes, though. It's a minor side effect of the spell."

Still glaring up at him, I lifted my hands up in an attempt levitate a large amount of dirt into the air to be thrown at him, yet nothing happened. The boy stood there calmly. I tried again, but still nothing happened.

"Are you trying to attack me?" he asked, puzzled. "Because you can't. See that little silver thing around your ankle?"

He pointed at the silver chain.

"It prevents its wearer from attacking the keeper of the chain."

I positioned my body and motioned my leg to sweep kick his ankles, but my foot stopped, only centimeters away. No matter how much I tried, I couldn't get any closer to him.

"Nice try," the boy said.

I dropped my foot. It was hopeless. My powers and ability to fight back were gone. I would have to negotiate. "What do you want from me? I don't have any money or anything of value, or anything that you could possibly want."

"I don't want your money even though you literally just cost me all of mine and some… point is, I'm not here to hurt you. I only said all of that stuff so that bunter would let us go. The last thing I want is to draw unwanted attention to myself."

"Then why did you try to help me?"

"I did help you, and besides, the last thing I also want is a dead person on my conscience."

"Mmm, I was caught off guard, first of all. And second, I can handle myself."

"Really? Before or after I just saved your life? Just checking for a friend."

"You know what, why don't you just let me go before I find a way give you another black eye, magic chain or no magic chain."

"Trust me." He knelt down beside me. "That was my intention before you gave me the first one."

He leaned towards me with his hand reaching for the chain. He caught a glance of my eyes, then his mouth nearly dropped and his hands fell to his side.

"What?" I asked. "Why are you looking at me like that?"

I turned my head to see if there was something or someone else behind me. It was just us. "What are you staring you at?" I asked.

"Cassie?" he finally whispered.

"Wait, what? Whose Cassie?" I asked, confused. I looked over my shoulder again, but again it was just us. "We're the only ones here."

"Your eyes," he said.

"So? What about them?"

"They're golden?"

"What? What does that have to do with anything? You said you would let me go, remember?"

"Humor me, for saving your life."

"Again, I can save my own life. That sorcerer just caught me off guard."

"Fine. Humor me for assisting you. Your eyes, are they naturally that color?"

"What?"

"Do psychics have some strange way of changing their eye color or something?"

"The color of my eyes are none of your business."

"I see."

"So, are you going to take this thing off or what?"

"Actually, on second thought, I think that I have changed my mind."

He stood back up.

"What do you mean that you've changed your mind!? You can't do that!" I stood up and faced him. He was about half a foot taller than me, and I didn't like it. I looked up into his eyes and said, "Let me go. Right. Now!"

He looked down at me with one eye brow raised and said, "Trust me, it's a lot safer in here than out there."

I opened the palms of my hands that laid at my side, and once again, I levitated the rocks and dirt that sat on the ground behind me up into the air and shot them towards the boy. He casually crossed his arms and watched as the rocks and the dirt hit another invisible wall just inches from his face.

I gazed down at my palms. "Dammit!" I yelled.

He just stood there with a condescending smirk across his face.

"No matter how many times you try, it won't work. You're still wearing the chain, remember?"

"Look." I sighed. "You sick psychopath, let me know go or else I will most definitely find a way to hurt you in the actual worst way possible."

"Uh huh. So, I'm going to go make some food."

"No, you're not," I said. "You're going to let me go, right now! Or—"

"Or?"

"My parents are going to come looking for me. All of them, my entire family. They'll find me, and then you'll be sorry!"

"Good luck. I've spent a lot of time crafting this dome. It's invisible, unless they have a wand."

"A wha—?" What the Hell was a wand? I've never read about that. Some weird sorcerer trick?

He smirked again. "Didn't think so."

A pit emerged at the bottom of my stomach.

The boy turned from me and started to walk away.

"Feel free to roam, walk around, or do whatever you want. I really don't care."

"YOU CAN'T KEEP ME HERE! I'LL ESCAPE! I'll—" But I couldn't finish the sentence. I felt as if all of the air had been sucked from my lungs, as his words began to sink in. My ankles weakened, and I fell back onto the ground, landing on both my butt and the bottom of my palms.

My parents were right. Hannah was right. They were all right. The realization paralyzed my throat.

I pulled my legs closer towards me. I sunk my chin into my knees, closed my eyes, and whispered, "Come find me, Hannah. Come find me."

To my dismay, I remained trapped in the invisible dome all day and into the night. I I kept to myself, sitting alone on the ground, with only the song of crickets to keep me company. The air was cold. I hugged my jacket closer to my skin. The sky was lit by the many stars scattered across it, complete with a shining crescent moon.

Although I kept hoping to think of a way to escape, no idea came to mind. Even the voice... *Wait, what happened to the voice?* I checked my pockets and saw that the locket was gone. Where was it?

I spread out my fingers, but still I couldn't sense its metallic texture. I must have dropped it somewhere when that other sorcerer attacked. It was the only person, or I suppose the only thing, that was honest with me. Then again, it plagued my mind for weeks with its voice, and that nightmare. I shuttered at the memory of the tunnel and the woman lying inside it. Maybe it was a good thing? I felt crazy with it in my head. At least, now my thoughts had returned back to normal. Or maybe it was just all in my head? Maybe I truly did just let my imagination have its way with me? In my own frustration, I laced my fingers through the hair on top of my head, and buried my face into my knees.

The locket was beautiful, though. And with it being hidden, I was sure that it would be a while before my parents would notice that it was missing. Still, I had hoped that it wasn't some family heirloom or something. I didn't need any additional misdeeds added to the list. Actually, the more I thought about it, the more I realized that the location of the locket probably didn't matter in comparison to my current circumstances.

The boy approached me. "Hey, are you sure that you don't want any?"

He held a plate of fish that he had fried in a pan over a fire in one hand and a cup of water in the other. This was probably the fourth time that he had offered me food, and each time I had silently refused.

I turned my head away.

"You know, it's really good. I'm going to take a wild guess here and say that you probably haven't eaten all day," he said.

I kept my head turned. The boy sat down beside me. I scooted over to my right, ensuring the distance between us.

"Look, I'm not going to hurt you. The sorcerers out here are dangerous. They, or…I guess we… kill our own kind, so imagine what they would do to you, a moving target."

"Moving target?" I grumbled. I pulled my knees in closer up to my chest. I stared down at the bending strips of grass.

"You don't know these people, their mannerisms, the way they walk, talk, think, or even dress. Not to mention, that you stick out like a sore thumb," the boy said.

"No, I don't! For all you know I could have been a sorceress."

"You're wearing purple pants. Bright purple pants."

"So? What does that have to do with anything?"

"First of all, normally only nobility or the wealthy pretending that they are nobility wear that color, and if you were a woman of nobility, then you would be wearing a dress and not pants. Second, if you were of nobility, then you would not be wandering the woods by yourself, because it makes you stick out like a purple pixie. You have no one. And lastly, you probably would have shown or done some type of magic to tell the bunter that you're one of us. You didn't do that. You ran."

That word, again. Bunter? What is a bunter? Ugh. It did not matter.

"Well, that's stupid. All of those are just assumptions. What if I just so happened to be a sorceress that just likes to wear pants?" I sighed. "So, that's it, then? You just plan on trying to keep me here?"

"Of course not. But if you really insist on leaving then you'll need new clothes. That way you will at least draw less attention to yourself. You don't want another bunter trying to kill or capture you, again."

"What is a bunter, anyway?" I asked.

"It's short for bounty hunter."

"So, sorcerers do actually want to hunt and kill us all down like animals?" I asked. My parents were right, again. My arms squeezed my legs, tighter.

"Huh? No. What? I don't know anyone that specifically goes out looking to hunt down and kill your kind, but yeah if someone happens to stumble across you, then yeah, he'll try to kill or capture you. Most bounty hunters around are actually on the hunt for whoever some wealthy nobleman wants to capture or something. It's nothing that you or I have to worry about."

My nerves slightly eased. I popped up. I looked over at the boy. He was now grinning at me. I turned away and looked back down at my knees.

"Are you sure you don't want any food?" he asked.

I laid my chin on my knees.

"I'm not lying when I say that it's good," he said.

The boy dangled the food in front of me.

It smelled delicious. The fish was hot, with the steam still rising from it. It was speckled with black dots, and held an aroma of sweet and salted spices that I had never smelled or seen before. My stomach rumbled. I clenched my jaw and fastened my lips tighter. I couldn't let him see that I was actually starving.

"I promise it's not poison or anything, or else I wouldn't be eating it," he said.

My stomached rumbled louder.

"Okay," he smirked.

He sat the plate and the cup down next to me.

"I'm just going to leave this here." He stood up and walked away.

I waited until he was gone before I looked at the plate and cautiously picked it up. It was still warm. As the aroma of the fish filled my nose, my mouth watered. I hovered one hand over the fish. I couldn't feel anything suspicious, such as poison; a trait my mother had taught me. I looked over to my right, and then to my left. When I saw that he wasn't watching, I bit into the fish with my entire mouth. "Ahhh! Hot!" I yelped.

I opened my mouth and let the fish ball back onto the plate. The roof of my mouth burned, and something small, thin, and lean was sticking to it. I pulled it out, and of course it was a fish bone.

I grabbed the cup of water and drank it quickly in attempts to soothe my mouth. For a few moments, it seemed like I couldn't bring myself to stop drinking the water. I sat the cup down and looked down at the plate.

I began to eat the fish, again. I broke the fish into other smaller pieces with telekinesis, and then levitated them into my mouth. The fish was moist, soft, and spicy. With each bite it took a few seconds for the full heat of the spices to kick in, and each time that it did, I coughed and took a sip of water. My taste buds tingled from the different array of flavors ranging from hot to sweet. This was in large contrast to the food back home. Our food was always bland, lumpy, and most of the time dry, except for oatmeal. I levitated the bone out of the rest of the fish and placed it back onto the plate. I finished the fish and drank the rest of the water.

The howling of wolves echoed around us. My eyes darted to the right and over to the left. Although their voices were loud, I did not see them.

"Don't worry."

I jumped. I turned around, and saw the boy standing behind me. I was relieved that it was only him, but then that relief turned into annoyance because it was him.

"Invisible dome, remember? They and no one else can see us," he said.

"Oh, because that makes me feel so safe," I said, sarcastically.

"Funny, but I just wanted to let you know that there is a sleeping bag over there," He pointed to his right. "If you want to use it. I will be on the other side, if you need me. I didn't put the fire out just in case you want to stay up late or want to use it so, don't forget to put out it before you go to sleep. Okay?"

The boy turned.

"Wait!" I called.

He stopped. "What is it?"

He did not turn around back around. I saw only saw the back of his head.

"Exactly how long do you plan on keeping me here?" I asked.

"We'll go into town tomorrow to get you some new clothes. After that, you can do or go wherever you want."

I was still puzzled. "Why are you doing this, again? I already told you that I don't have any money."

"I suppose my mother taught me to always help someone who is in need."

"I didn't need your help."

"Well, you're not dead, are you? And besides, you will still need a disguise."

He walked away. I watched him pull out a small woven sack from his pocket and from inside the sack, he pulled out a large blue blanket that clearly was more than fifty times the size of the sack. He proceeded to pull out a pillow and small square cloth. My eyes widened in amazement. At first, I couldn't understand how that was even possible, but then I rolled my eyes and thought to myself, *'Magic.'*

He whispered something while pointing at the cloth. It stiffened as if it were frozen, and then he placed it on the eye that I punched as he laid down onto his back.

Strange. I had spent most of the day around him, even if I was not interacting with him. While he did not have a rasp in his voice, and his voice was not as deep as the other sorcerer, he spoke with the same smoothness and vowel emphasis. *It must be their accent.*

I laid down onto my back in the grass.

"Ow!" Something pricked me in the back of my head. I reached behind, and felt the rose pin on the hair band that Hannah had given me. "Oh."

I had almost forgotten about it. I readjusted my ponytail and laid my head back down. I gazed back up at the moon and the stars in the sky. They were beautiful. My thoughts drifted off to a time in which I longed for a night in which I could truly sleep underneath real stars; however, tonight I longed for the ugly misshaped stars that were in my bedroom.

I wanted to see steel walls and to hear the voices of my family.

I sighed. I could only imagine their reactions when they must have realized that I was gone. And, Hannah…most of the time, I had hated when she was right. However, this time I was frightened.

"I'm sorry, Hannah. I'm sorry, Mom. I'm sorry, Dad," I whispered.

ASHWOOD

"Hey, wakey wakey."

The boy stood over me as I laid in the sleeping the bag.

"Ugh." My voice was groggy. I groaned and turned over.

"Come on, you have to get up. We're going into town. It'll be fun," he said.

"Maybe for you."

"Hey, the faster we go into town, the faster we get you actual sorcerer clothes, and then the faster you can leave, unless you've forgotten already?" The boy walked over to the other side of me.

"Well, you have magic. Just conjure up something and then let me go."

He raised one eyebrow. "Yeah, no. That is not how magic works."

"My dad can make things out of nowhere."

"What?" The boy took a step back. He met my eyes, and titled his head slightly to the side. "How is that possible?"

"I mean, psychics or I guess some psychics can do that, I think. He can. I can't. And Mom can't. He's trying to teach my sister, but I haven't really met anyone else other than—" I hesitated. It was like my tongue was almost embarrassed to say the next few words, especially while staring at someone whom I assumed was used to being around other people. "My family," I said, softly.

His posture relaxed, and he sighed. "Oh."

The boy nearly half-smiled. "Psychic. That makes sense."

"What?"

"Nothing. I almost forgot. I haven't met many psychics in person. Clearly psychics and sorcerers are different. I can't just make something out of nothing."

"But last night I saw you pull out a blanket from a small bag that was clearly was a lot smaller than the actual blanket. How was that possible, if you can't conjure things out of nothing?"

He chuckled. "I keep the sack for storage. I didn't make any of the things inside it."

"Oh." Magic was different. Very different.

"Yeah, so let's go," the boy said.

"Wait. How do I know that you'll actually take off the chain this time?"

"Honestly, I have no reason to keep you here."

"Fine." I sighed. I sat up and stretched my arms out as I yawned. "Food?"

"We'll get some in town."

"I hate you."

"Well, we'll call it even for yesterday."

"Ha. I did do a good job, now didn't I?" I grinned as I looked up at his bruised eye.

"Alright, smartass." He took the tiny woven sack from his pants pocket, and reaching inside, he pulled out a large, rolled-up hooded cape that must have been about forty sizes larger than the sack. I watched in astonishment.

"Try not to look so surprised at everything or else this is never going to work."

He tossed me the hooded cape.

"Put it on. It should be able to hide your clothes."

I stood up with the cape and wrapped it around myself. It was a heavy, thick brown fabric. The cape was mostly smooth, but had random patches of itchy rugged fabric along the inside of sleeves towards the bottom of them that brushed up against my wrists. It held the scent of both the dirt and burnt tree bark. The bottom of the cape dragged on the ground, and the end of sleeves reached several inches passed my hands. "Good enough," he said.

The boy reopened his sack.

"*Apudo!*" he said.

All of the camping equipment was sucked into the sack.

"Wow." My eyes widened as I watched.

"C'mon, let's go." He began to walk away.

"But, the—" I began, pointing at the invisible dome.

"It's gone. Come on."

We walked through the forest for about an hour, until we reached a wooden archway with the word *ASHWOOD* carved into its center in large bold letters. We walked through the archway and entered into busy a village. There were rows of small wooden and stone bungalows, and market stalls filled with sorcerers. The roofs of the housing varied from some being made of wood or stone to golden straws of hay to some sort of round, red plated structure, midway between dirt and stone. The booths were encased in different colors from bright blue to greens to pinks to yellows that glowed in the distance from the fabrics, jewels, and trinkets that they carried. Pockets of hordes of sorcerers stood next to them, different men and women of varying sizes. Some were young. Others were old. Some carried infants and children, while others were by themselves. Their faces also varied in numerous expressions. They ranged from smiles to frowns to inquisition to anger. They all chatted, filling the atmosphere with laughter, whispers, and yells. The streets were crowded. Everyone walked in their own separate directions, frequently bumping into both us or each other.

Boom!

I looked over to my left. Only a few feet away, wedged in between two stands, blue smoke rose up, and from it appeared an older sorcerer in earthy brown and dingy green robes down to his brown boots. He was short and pale, with white hair that seeped from his burlap cap and a long white beard that stretched down to his chest.

"Come one, come all," he said as he spread out his arms. *"Numatas!"*

Five small cloth puppets of silver knights on top of gray, brown, and white clothed horses appeared in the air and swirled around him. The knights held long, golden, slender fabric poles.

"Come hear the valiant tales of the knights of Oswald and their defeat of the Ice Dragon!" His voice roared in between speech and song as he turned the heads of curious children.

Four of the puppets centered around one puppet. They charged and attacked their victim, stabbing it with their poles. The poor puppet combusted into pink, red, blue, yellow, and purple shreds of paper. Both the children and I gasped in amazement. Such a spectacle! Some of the children giggled, while others seemed to be unable to close their mouths. Yet, all of the adults paid the sorcerer no mind. They continued their talking or purchasing their goods, as if he was not there.

I looked further at the other sorcerers. Many of the men and boys had hair around the same length as my kidnapper, or at longest to the tips of their shoulders. They ranged in curl patterns from ringlets to as straight as a bow staff. Some wore burlap shirts and pants, while others donned fancier garments in the form of robes, like the old, bearded, storyteller.

Most of the sorceress women were fancier with their hair, wearing elegant curls or fancy thick crowned braids. Their hair also ranged from tightly coiled ringlets to straight. Many of the young girls that I could see wore their hair down, some with the crowned braids on top of their heads, others with thick loosely braids that hanged down along their free unbraided hair, while others just let their hair fall naturally into a loose ponytail. It was only the very small girls who had braided pigtails. Similar to the sorcerer men, the fabric of their dresses, and capes ranged from that same burlap to a softer and more elegant fabric of different colors including blues, pinks, and at times purples. Despite the differences in fabric, and at times detail, most of the gowns featured skirts that went down to their ankles, long sleeves that flared out at the ends, and either corseted strings or buttons in the front from their chests to their waists.

"Okay, so I believe it's this way," the boy said.

"Wait, what?" I looked back at him.

"This way!" He pointed diagonally to the right down the path of stands and other sorcerers.

"Let's go." He gently tugged my chain forward.

As we continued to walk, I noticed that the air was filled with a mixture of new and intriguing scents and fragrances. Some good, like the scents from the nectar of flowers in the forest, and others bad, worse than the smell of garbage.

A gust of wind circled around me, carrying a golden dust that sparkled in the sunlight. I stopped as it continued to dance around my face, down to my stomach, and then back to its owner – a sorcerer at one of the stands to our right.

He had light green eyes and chestnut hair. He was tall and slim. His stand was decorated with rainbow-colored transparent bottles and vials.

"Potions and new charms for the pretty young girl, extracted from the nectar of fresh flowers," he said.

I gazed over at him.

"Or maybe some of our new creams to brighten up your face to potential young suitors, hmm?" he asked.

He opened a vial, and the sweet scent of wild lilies tickled my nose.

"Sorry, not interested," the boy said.

The boy grabbed my wrist and said, "Come on."

He pulled me forward as we walked. I snatched my hand away and asked, "Whoa, what is your problem? What was that for!?"

"I'm not trying to be forceful, but some of the stands here are just scams, and we don't know that person. Also, again," he leaned into my ear and whispered, "you really do have to stop looking so mesmerized by magic. It will tip people off."

He pointed at many large men who uniformly wore pieces of silver and blue armor, swords around their waists, and the outline of a yellow crown that sat on the chest plate of their armor. They appeared to be travelling in pairs. Some walking along the streets like us, and others just standing by the different stands and bungalows.

"Who are they?" I asked.

"Don't look at them. If they look at you, look down. Otherwise, just look forward and keep walking." He followed his own advice, avoiding all eye contact with them.

We continued to walk as he continued to speak in a hushed voice. "They are foot soldiers placed here to keep the peace, but you have to be careful around them. They're normally bored, and are the ones who actually cause the trouble that they are supposed to prevent...actually, wait. This way."

We walked off the road and up to a wooden pole.

"Is something wrong?" I asked.

"Nothing. I just want you stay right here."

"What? What do you mean?"

"Just stay here and look normal. *Involvente pole!*"

The other end of the chain that he carried disappeared from his possession and reappeared at the bottom of the pole.

"What are you doing?" I asked.

"I'll be right back."

"You can't leave me here!"

"Calm down, you'll be fine."

"No! What if another bunter comes!? And—" I began. My heart raced.

"Hey. Hey. Hey..." he interrupted. He stepped closer and whispered, "...if you just act natural, nothing bad will happen. There is no bunter here. No one is after you."

I looked around at the groups of sorcerers that passed by us. The tips of my nails went to my mouth.

He continued, "You're okay."

I looked back at him, unconvinced.

"You're going to be okay. Just try to stay calm, and keep your voice down."

"But—"

"You'll be fine. Trust me."

"And, if I don't?"

"Don't really have a choice. Relax. I will be right back. You will be fine." The boy stepped away.

I stood there, angrily watching the boy vanish into the crowd, until...

"Ow!"

The edge of something went into my forehead. My hands went to my forehead and I looked up. It was a blue jay. Wait, no. It wasn't a blue jay. It was blue paper in the form of a tiny bird, flying and chirping on its own.

"My bird!"

A little boy with curly, sand-colored hair and dark blue robes ran up to me. He looked around the age of seven. He had bright blue eyes and a raw sienna complexion. He kept jumping up and down, reaching for the bird.

"Sorry. It wasn't supposed to do that, but I almost got it!" he said.

"Haylan!" A sorceress woman approached.

She wore a long, sky-blue, corseted gown that nearly sparkled in the light. Draped over her shoulders was a loose, dark velvet cape at her shoulders. Like the boy, her eyes were blue, and her hair was the same texture; however, her hair was black, pinned back, and reached well past her shoulders. She had smooth skin, accompanied by a stern look upon her face. The sorceress extended her hand. *"Capara parchment!"*

The bird flew to the palm of her open hand. She grabbed the wrist of her son with her other hand. "Haylan, apologize," said the sorceress.

"My apologies, miss," the boy said.

"It's okay," I said. My voice was shakier than I had anticipated. Why was I so nervous? It was just a child and his mother, just like my family. Then it dawned on me. *I had never met another family before.*

Her face relaxed into a friendly smile. "I also apologize. Children, what a handful they are. I would rather tame a group of unruly pixies sometimes."

I smiled weakly.

"Come, Haylan. We mustn't be late to meet your betrothed. You're always playing with that thing without knowing how to properly control it," the sorceress said. She and her son turned and walked away.

I told myself to calm down. Admittedly, I was a little confused. I looked around at the hustle and bustle of merchants and other sorcerers around me. There were other kids running and playing, while the adults talked and shopped for goods at the stands. The bunter I had encountered yesterday was dangerous. However, maybe not everyone was? Huh. Dad never came back harmed from the outside. My face relaxed into a warm smile.

"Free sample from the Boar's Tavern," a voice spoke from behind.

I turned around and saw a short, round sorcerer carrying a silver tray of small samples of meat with tiny picks of wood stuck in the middle of them.

"Compliments of our tavern. We're open all day." He motioned the tray towards me.

Should I?

They smelled so good, and I hadn't eaten yet. Normally, Mom had food fixed right when Hannah and I woke up every morning. I could feel my stomach rumble, and the inside of my mouth water. My hand cautiously hovered over the tray. Should I taste it? Hmm, I don't see why not.

"Watch out!"

The boy reappeared right next to me.

"*Vyni!*" he said.

The chain went back to him.

"We have to go, now!" he said.

"There! There's the fuckin' beggar!"

A soldier pointed at us.

"What's going on!?" I asked.

"Don't worry about it. Come on!" he said.

He grabbed my wrist and we both began to run. More and more soldiers joined in on the chase, until there were seven of them behind us.

"What did you do?" My voice was frantic.

I looked back at the soldiers as they chased us. My heart began to pound, and goosebumps rose on the back of my neck. The boy led me into the crowds as we pushed through the villagers. We ran in and out of the alleys between the lodges, and jumping over piles of hay and garbage.

"Where are we going!?" I asked, panting.

"Just follow me!"

Corner after corner after corner, we turned. Different-colored spells and blasts flew at us; some green, some blue, some gray. Screams and shrieks filled the crowd. Some froze, while others scrambled to get out of the way. The boy and I ducked. We dodged as we ran, until we reached another back alley, shaded by the shadows of the walls it cut in between. We pressed our backs against the wall, and watched the soldiers run pass us. By this point, my heart both screamed through my ear drums and was nearly jumping out of my chest. I closed my fists and pressed them further into the wall to prevent my hands from shaking.

"Seriously, what did you do?" I asked.

"Shhh."

"Do you hear something?" I whispered. I looked back and forth.

"No."

My eyes travelled back to him. He whispered, "I just want you to be quiet."

"I don't see—"

"Duck!" the boy said.

A soldier appeared from behind us and fired off a spell. Quickly, we crouched down, as it flew past our heads and collided into the wall, creating a loud rumble.

"Are you okay?" he asked.

I nodded, yes.

The boy took my hand, and we ran back into the street. We stopped, surrounded on all sides by now eight soldiers, including the one that had just attacked us.

"Detra A—" they all began to say, but the boy cut them off.

"Fumus!"

Instantly, the area filled with a thick gray smoke, making it both hard to see and to breathe.

"Transmedo!" the boy said.

As before, all of the colors of the area began to blend together, as my body was being sucked forward. We vanished, and then reappeared on top of the slanted brown-plated roof on one of the lodges. At first disoriented, I stretched out my arms to regain balance. My hands traveled to my stomach to soothe its unease.

"Get down!" whispered the boy.

He was already ducked down, using the slanted roof as a cover. I joined him. We stared down at the smoke.

"I'll be right back," he said.

I grabbed his wrist. "You can't leave me here with all of those sorcerers down there! What if they..."

My voice was frantic.

"It's okay. I have an idea on how to get them off our trail. I'm not going to leave you up here. I promise," he said.

I didn't want to let go of his wrist, but I did not have a choice. I doubted that I could stop him, and I did not want to be captured by the soldiers. I stared down at his wrist, then slowly released my grip on it.

"Hey," he said.

I looked up into his emerald eyes.

"I'll be back. I came back before. *Transmedo!*" The boy disappeared.

My eyes went back down towards the smoke. Flashes of green light appeared in different and various areas in the smoke. The boy reappeared next to me, coughing.

When the smoke started to clear, the soldiers started to scatter.

The boy closed his eyes, sighing in relief.

I stopped, motionless, as my senses began to trigger. I cupped my hands together. When I turned around, I met the eyes of a lone soldier, holding a sword in his hands, about to swing at the boy. I shot nearly all of my energy out through my hands, pushing the soldier backwards and off the roof.

The boy looked at me with widened eyes.

"You just—" he began.

"Up there!" a soldier shouted.

"Detra Arma!"

We crouched back down as more spells flew towards us. The boy placed his hand on top of mine and said, *"Transmedo!"*

We disappeared and reappeared on the ground behind the lodge. By this point, I was starting to feel increasingly dizzy. The buildings and ground moved in a circular motion, and my feet did not know where to steadily step. The boy grabbed my shoulders, keeping me from falling. He let go and took my hand. We ran. Again, we cut corners and ran through alleyways, every so often looking over our shoulders.

We reached a barn. Both of us looked around. There was no one. I sighed in relief. The boy and I turned around the barn's corner. We jumped back. We found ourselves cut off by two of the soldiers.

"Fotia!" said the soldier in front.

The boy pulled me closer to himself, and said, *"Aspedia!"*

He held out both of his palms, and moved in them both into a circular motion in the air, creating a round, lime-green transparent shield. The spell glowed bright green as it crashed into the shield. It pushed both of us back. I looked over at the boy and saw his face and body tense up while holding the shield. I lifted my hands up in front of my face to protect it from the hot sting of the spell that was bleeding through it.

"You have to run," the boy said.

"What?" I asked.

"I won't be able to hold this up much longer, and he is continuously putting more energy behind this spell."

Crack! Fractures in the shield began to appear and spread throughout it.

He continued: "On the count of three, I need you to run or jump out of the way, okay?"

I nodded, yes.

"Good…one…two…three!" the boy said.

As I leapt out of the way, the shield shattered. The boy was knocked back a few feet away and onto the ground.

"Get the girl!" said the soldier who had conjured the spell.

A devious smirk appeared on the other's face as he began to walk towards me. Time slowed, and the tiny hairs on the back of my neck rose. My chest pounded in pain, while my eyes darted around. There was nothing that I could use as a weapon. I jumped to my feet and ran as fast as I could.

I turned a corner around the barn. However, it only took two steps before I tripped over the silver chain around my ankle.

Damn!

I had almost forgotten that it was still wrapped around my ankle. I stood back up and pressed my body against the outside wall of the barn. My eyes searched for anything, tools, pieces of wood, anything. I noticed a broom lying against a fence that stood about a yard away. I stretched out my hand and levitated it towards me. I rolled up my sleeves and took the broom in my hands. I closed my eyes and silently waited.

The pitter-patter of footsteps emerged, while I stood in patience. When its owner turned the corner in my direction, I emerged with the broom in hand.

He attempted to cup his hands together, but I swirled the handle back and forth like in training, knocking him in the arms. Unable to keep his stance, he took a few steps back. He withdrew a sword from a scabbard around his waist. I used my gift to jolt the handle into his chest, and then shot it out of his hands and onto the ground by our side.

The sorcerer halted as he looked down at me. His eyes widened, but after a few seconds, his face relaxed into a sly grin. He vanished. I looked around, but I couldn't find him. I took a deep breath and closed my eyes. I used telekinesis to feel out the area.

There!

I opened my eyes. I was about turn around when the sorcerer hit me at an angle in between my back and my side.

"Ahhh!" I yelped.

The broom was knocked out of my hands, and I fell to the ground. My hand went to my side as I held in more screams. My other hand clutched the ground, as I leaned forward.

Get up! Remember your training!

The sorcerer stood over me and cupped his hands together, palms out and facing towards me. As he began to say, *"Detra A—"*

I shot my hand up and used telekinesis to throw the dirt and dust from the ground into his eyes. He stopped mid-word, and his hands went up to his face. I kicked his ankles with a sweep. He fell backwards and hit his head on a rock. I stood up. Although my back and side still hurt, I could move them. I levitated the broom back to me. I flipped it upside down, pointing the top of the broom handle at the sorcerer's neck.

The pitter-patter of more footsteps emerged. I drew my attention back towards the corner, with the broom firmly in hand, when the boy dashed towards me.

"Hey, whoa," he said, off guard. His eyes went from me to the fallen soldier. "Well, aren't you full of surprises. Impressive."

"I told you before, I was only caught off guard."

He stepped towards me, but I took a step back.

"Do you want to stay here and wait for more to come?" he asked.

I lowered the broom.

"Thought so," the boy said.

He walked up to me, took my hand, and said, *"Transmedo!"*

We vanished, but left the broom.

SYCHE!

We reappeared in the midst of more bungalows and cottages. By the third time, I think my stomach was starting to get used to the teleporting, but my dizziness was not quite there yet. The boy caught my shoulders before I had a chance to fall.

"Whoa," I said.

"Are you okay?" he asked.

"No," I mumbled.

He smirked.

When the ground and buildings stopped spinning, I asked "So, where are we now?"

"Brusnick, a village over." He let go of my shoulders.

"Wait, hold on. You mean that you could have teleported us to a different a village this entire time?"

"It's more complicated than that."

"How the Hell is it more complicated!?"

"Look, magic is energy, and energy is traceable. Before, it was a group of soldiers and us. If we had teleported, then it wouldn't have been hard for them figure out which energy source did not belong to them, and they would have followed us here. That's why I teleported back down from the roof in the first place to shoot out random spells. I tried to muddy our tracks. But just now, we were only down to two men, which we both disoriented. By the time they come to, the magic trail will be cold, making it harder for them to track us, and we will either have enough time to leave this place unnoticed or to at least blend in with the crowd."

"I suppose that makes sense."

"Yeah. Now, c'mon."

"To where?"

"You're still hungry, aren't you?"

Finally! I exclaimed eagerly to myself. Yet, I mumbled grumbly: "Fine."

I followed him to another barn. It was connected to a larger wooden and gray stone building. He tried to open it, but the sliding door was locked.

"I thought that you said that we were getting food?" I asked.

"We are."

"In here?"

"You ask a lot of questions."

"I'm sorry. I'm constantly being dragged off to somewhere that I don't know, so I think that the least you can do is answer a few questions."

He turned his attentions back to the door.

"*Apierto!*" he said.

However, the door still did not open.

"Shit," he mumbled. "The password, the password, the password. Yes, got it. *Patenti!*"

Password? *He has been here before.*

The door opened.

"Come in," he said.

We stepped inside. There were bushels of hay stacked up against the walls and loose hay scattered all long the floor. My nose twitched at the mixture of strange smells. The walls and pillars were built only of wood. Straight ahead was a latter that led to an open second floor filled with even more bales of hay.

The boy pulled the small sack from his pocket and opened it. He reached his arm inside and pulled out a heap of rolled-up tan and brown fabric. He tossed it to me.

"What is this?" I asked as I caught it.

"A dress. To help you blend in?"

I held it up. It was large, full in skirt, and had long sleeves with a small flare at the ends. The dress bore a faded cloth-like corset that was laced with string, and the fabric of the skirt was heavier and tougher than any dress that I had ever worn.

He pointed behind me. "There is a closet over there where you can change."

Another, much smaller door swung open from the inside, and

standing in its doorway was a young bar maiden. She had big blue eyes. Her long, thick, black hair was pinned back with large loose curls. She wore a long faded red dress that looked as if it had been washed too many times, with a light tan apron soiled with flour over it. The fabric at the ends of her sleeves and at her feet were frayed. Her waist was slim, yet her chest and hips curved out. I looked down at my chest. My bust wasn't nearly as big, but still sizable enough to cup into my hands, so I suppose that's something.

"Hey, who are you!?" She turned her head and saw the boy. "Gre…Grey, what are you doing here, and who is this girl!?"

"I can explain," he said.

"If my mistress comes back to see this—" she continued.

"I promise you she won't," he interrupted. "We just had a bit of a run in with the law and just a need a quick place to restock on some food."

Her faced relaxed into a smile. "Up to your old tricks, I see. Is that where you got your badge of honor around your eye?" The maiden glanced back at me. Her face turned in a snare and she crossed her arms. "So, who exactly is your new lady friend?"

"This is um, Cass. Cass, meet Ruby. Speaking of which, Ruby, you wouldn't happen to have any potions on hand that I could use for my eye, would you?" he asked.

Ruby turned her attentions back to the boy and answered, "'Fraid not."

"Ruby," he said.

"Always asking for favors. Even if I had some, you know that they are reserved for fights that happen in the pub. Besides, it doesn't look too bad."

She was right. The skin around his eye was discolored, with lines of purple and red around it, yet there wasn't any swelling, and he could open it just as well as his other eye.

"Anyway," Ruby looked back at me, "if you and um, Cass, are finished, I think it would be best that you leave before my mistress comes back."

"Can you give us a moment?" he asked.

"Oh sure, it's not like my neck isn't on the line or anything." Ruby stepped out, closing the door behind her.

"Sorry about that," he said. "But like I said, there is a closet over there where you can change."

I walked over to the closet. I looked back. He was standing quietly, with his head turned in the opposite direction. I faced forward and went into the closet. I closed the door, behind me, and was confronted with a mirror in front of me. I held the dress up to the mirror before taking in a deep breath. "Here we go," I whispered.

As I took off my jacket and pajamas, I noticed petite red marks towards my back. I turned around in the mirror to see more. They were small red lines and pricks spaced out, all along it. I gasped.

They weren't fresh. Maybe, a few days old. Thus, they couldn't have been from sleeping on the ground last night. *Odd.*

"How did—" I began.

"Hey Cass, not trying to rush you, but we don't know when Ruby is coming back."

"Oh, right," I said, startled.

I slipped on the dress and came out of the closest with my pajamas and jacket folded in my arms. Despite the extra folds of fabric tightly hugging my waist, the bust and the stomach felt loose. The strings seemed to sewn into the dress, so they did not hang in front of me. The collar slanted a little to my left shoulder. Even the bottom of the skirt relaxed itself onto the floor. I wiggled a little, attempting to find some type of comfort in these strange clothes. I laid my right arm on top of my left arm, as they both grabbed the other's elbow. At least the fabric was thicker. I would not have to wear the jacket to stay warm as I did with the pajamas.

The boy turned back around and faced me.

"I'm sure Ruby has some sort of clothes-fitting spell that you can use." He walked up to me. He took the pajamas and jacket out of my arms and placed them into his sack. It swallowed them seamlessly.

"Wow. I still can't get over that," I said.

"We don't want to leave any evidence of us being here. Now, your ankle."

"What?" I asked.

"Relax, I'm not going to do anything. Just show me your ankle."

I pulled skirt of the dress up, just enough to expose my ankles. The boy extended the palm of his right hand down towards my ankle with the charm and whispered something.

The chain unwrapped itself and shot to his hand.

"You're letting me go?" I let go of the dress.

"Well, we did have a deal."

"And you're actually keeping your word?"

"Yeah, why wouldn't I?"

"Well, considering this whole situation is your fault," I said, awkwardly.

He smirked. "Not arguing with that."

The door swung open, with Ruby behind it. Both of our heads snapped towards her. Ruby leaned against the doorframe and carelessly twiddled with the tips of her fingers in front of her face.

"Hey, so I just thought that you two otta' know that there are guards searching the outside surrounding area, right now," she said.

Guards? My stomach dropped at the news, and my hands went into my forehead. "You cannot be serious."

"'Fraid so," Ruby said.

I sighed and shook my head. Just when I was finally free. This was my luck.

"You owe me for this one, Grey." Ruby turned towards him. "I told one of them that I have never seen you a day in my life."

"So, you're going to let us stay, aren't you?" he asked.

"Not in here, you're not. My mistress finds you two, and then all three of us will be thrown out. Just follow me and keep your head down," she said.

"Great. A table in the back should suffice," he said.

Ruby began walking. I still stood in silent disbelief of our situation.

"Well?" she asked. "C'mon now. I haven't got all day before I actually do throw you both out!"

"Hold on." The boy extended his hand out towards the closet. *"Capara hooded cape!"*

Oops, I forgot the cape.

The boy's brown hooded cape flew from the floor of the closet into the boy's hand. "Okay. Let's go."

We followed Ruby out of the barn and into its connected building.

Inside the dining the area, the air was warm and filled with the scent of freshly baked dough, hot spices and meats. Sorcerers and sorceresses sat at their respective tables drinking colored ales and liquids. Some of the glasses and cups sat on their tables, while others magically hovered next to their faces. There was a mixture of laughter, chatter, and a few pockets of sorrow.

Amongst the chatter were words that I recognized; couples or friends talking about their day, while others spoke words that I could not recognize. A few of their words sounded familiar to the words of their spells. The most confusing ones were the conversations that contained both casual conversation and magic words themselves.

Beneath the chatter was a thin layer of music that filled the air. Quick and cheery in pace, and with a soft lower beat. Far off to the other side of the space were floating wooden instruments that played by themselves. One was a small and cylindrical, with holes on the top of it. I assumed a flute or something similar. Another was large and round, with a long flat piece of wood stretching from its mid-section to beyond the top of the body of the instrument itself. It had thin strings that were moving on their own. A cello, I guessed.

Lastly, next to it was another miniature version of the large round instrument, except this one had a stick or something playing the strings instead of the strings playing themselves. Either a violin or a fiddle. I didn't know the difference. I had never seen instruments in person. I had only seen pictures and briefly read about characters' interacting or hearing them in tales or adventures of others stories. My breath nearly paused in delight. I just realized I had never heard live music before. I smiled.

It was beautiful.

The room was lit by the sunlight from the windows. There were floating candles right next to each window, though none of them were lit. Like the instruments, all of the tables, chairs, and even the floor boards were made of wood.

On each table were petite glass vases no larger than your average glass cup. In their mouths were three glowing, five-lobed leaves, with stems that stretched to the bottom of the vase. The leaves ranged in color from yellow to deep red. After a few seconds, each leaf would transition into a new color within that spectrum.

"Wow," I whispered. My eyes were mesmerized. It was the beauty of autumn captured and contained in a vase.

As we continued to walk, the floor boards made a strange moaning sound with nearly every step. I looked down at the floor boards as I cautiously took my next step. They creaked again.

"If there is food or something on the floor, just step over it," Ruby said.

I looked back up to find both the boy and Ruby a little ahead of me. They both stopped and looked back over their shoulders at me. The boy appeared puzzled, while Ruby looked at me with arms folded, one eyebrow raised, and a frown sketched across her face.

I nodded in agreement, although there was nothing on the floor. I caught back up to them, and we all continued walking through the tavern.

"Are you okay?" The boy leaned towards me and whispered into my ear.

"Yup." I gently bit my bottom lip. I supposed I was making it a little too obvious that I did not belong. I had to act like none of this was new, yet how could I, when all of it was more imaginative than any of the scenes from my books? I took a deep breath, attempting to freeze my face, calm.

Along the walls was a straight line of framed rectangular paintings and black and white sketches. The frames were made of bundled twigs and small branches of wood, intertwined into each other like vines along the borders of each painting. Their colors ranged from cool lilac, blue, and green to vivid colors of orange, yellow, and red. They were pictures of various flowers, orchids, rose bushes, and petunias. The sketches were done in charcoal, seemingly the same materials that Hannah and Mom had used in their artwork. These sketches portrayed subjects from nature such as birds, fruit, and trees along prairies.

Straight ahead to the back wall was another piece of framed artwork, except this one was much bigger than the rest. It was a portrait of an older gentleman, facing forward. The subject held an astringent expression. He stood tall, with long, straight blonde hair that was nearly white, neatly slicked back to his shoulders. His eyes were strikingly blue, and he wore dark blue robes with deep red buttons and trimmings. The amount of detail reminded me of the portrait that my mother had painted of our family. However, the colors in this painting were cold and dark. The colors in our family portrait were more vibrant.

"Cass—" the boy gently placed his hand on my shoulder.

"What?" I asked.

"We're at the table," he said.

"Oh, yeah. I just thought that I saw something. It was nothing," I said.

"Oookay?"

We sat down. The boy put his hooded cape in the seat next time him, while I sat across from him. The table was small and round, but it seated four people. He looked over at Ruby and said, "We'll take two waters and your best house sandwiches."

"Mardere me," she scowled as she walked away.

"What does that mean?" I asked.

He shook his head. "Don't worry about it."

"No really, what's with her?"

"Eh, it's a long story. We may or may have dated, but it was a long time ago."

"Nice going," I scoffed. He was a typical boy in bad, boring romance novels.

"Hey, it was a long time ago, and only a few dates. This is still the safest place we could be. She won't turn us in."

"How do you know?"

"Because people you can trust are very hard to come by out here, so you don't get rid of the ones that you do."

"Really?" I folded my arms.

"What?" he asked.

"Oh, nothing."

"Look, you can trust me too. I'm not saying that what I did was right, but at least I did have good intentions."

"You keep saying that I can trust you, but you never even told me your name, Grey or why the guards were chasing us."

He smirked. "My name is Grey. And I may or may not have taken the dress while a merchant wasn't looking."

"You stole it!"

"Keep your voice down! Are you trying to get us caught?"

I lowered my voice. "But, stealing is—"

"How else did you expect to get clothes to blend in? You cost me all of my money, remember?"

"Oh." I leaned back in the chair.

"If it will help, you can ask me more questions," he said.

"Well, what does the word 'syche' mean? Why did the bunter call me that? Does it mean psychic or something?"

Grey averted his eyes to the table and looked visibly uncomfortable when he said, "You could say that."

"And?"

"It's—" he began, but then he paused. "How do I say this? Not that I feel this way or anything, but it's basically a combination of the words psychic and a word from our old language, 'ches', which means slogas."

"What's a slogas?"

"Uh, it's not exactly the nicest term for someone that is not quite right in the head. You know sorcerers or others that aren't all there, mentally or developed from birth," he said.

"Oh, I see."

"Not a word that I'd ever use, but ya know."

Neither of us said anything, causing an awkward pause, until Ruby came back with two glasses of floating water at her side and two plates of chicken sandwiches. Grey looked at the sandwiches. His face lit up. "Thanks Ruby. Any chance that we can get some ale?"

"You are eating for free. Don't push it." The water and food gently lowered themselves onto the table in front of us and she walked away.

"Smooth," I said, sarcastically.

"Shut up," he said.

I snickered at him and turned my attention to the sandwich. The scent of the spices lifted from the plate and into my nose. I peeled the crust off the sandwich and sunk my teeth into it. The bread was thick, yet light. It was pale brown, and spiced with tiny black and green flakes on top. Between the slices of bread was a thin layer of grilled chicken and light yellow curdled chucks of some gooey substance. The chicken was sweet, but the yellow goo was bitter. The sandwich lit up my taste buds with overwhelming sensations of flavor.

I noticed Grey staring at me.

"What?" I asked.

"It's that good, huh?"

"You've never had psychic food before."

"You're not wrong."

A door opened and a sorcerer stumbled inside to the center of the pub. He swayed right and left with each step. He was bald on top, but had a grizzly brown beard with specks of white spread throughout it. His face and clothes were nearly covered in soot and dirt, and he wreaked of alcohol. "The psychics are comin'! The psychics are comin'!" he yelled.

Grey leaned in and whispered, "It's fine. Just act natural and ignore him. No one will know if we don't react."

"I won't freak out," I whispered. I kept my head down and stared at my sandwich. My shoulders tensed and my heart sped up. I stayed very still and did not look over at the sorcerer, but I could still hear him.

The chatter in the pub rose.

"One has already been spotted in the Arculus forest. They're invadin', I'm telling ye! They're invadin'! Hide yer—"

"That's enough!" Ruby's voice roared.

I turned my head.

Ruby walked up to the man. "I don't know what kind of trouble you're trying to start, but you're not going to start it here. Get out!"

"What are ye some psychic sympathiza'!? Ye trai—"

"I said that's enough!" Ruby held out her palms towards him and said, *"Ventus!"*

The drunkard flew backwards through the entrance and out into the streets.

"Claudere!" Ruby said, and the doors closed behind him.

She walked back up to Grey and I.

"The people I have to deal with," she groaned.

"You just kicked him out. I wouldn't worry about it," Grey said.

"Well, he's not the first, and certainly won't be the last." Ruby folded her arms and continued, "Apparently, there was a sighting yesterday, and everyone is going around talking about it like chickens with their heads cut off."

"What are they saying?" Grey asked.

"I don't know, something about some bunter killing a whole lot of them, but one getting away."

"Just rumors, I'm sure," Grey interrupted. He looked over at me and gave a subtle nod, I assumed as a sort of assurance.

I gave a slight nod back.

Ruby continued, "Probably, but then there was something about some broken silver locket that he tried to sell off. I know that's fake. What nobleman would part with such a thing unless it was a fake, or he stole it?"

Oh, no. The locket! I bit my bottom lip and closed my eyes for a few moments. It was a family heirloom, after all. "Dammit," I whispered.

Ruby kept talking. "He was arrested, of course. Ugh. I don't care, but the last thing that I need to be called is a syche sympathizer. Imagine me, a sympathizer to one of those disgusting, idiotic, nature-hating creatures, and then also to think about being ostracized on those false claims, especially when they are the ones that killed the late Prince Ignius. Our dear sweet loyalist prince. Which reminds me, I hear that he was quite attractive, at least way more attractive than anyone in this forsaken place, from the way his portraits were described. I wouldn't have minded having any of his...well, doesn't matter now. But still, to think of all that, and then have someone call you the risk of being called a syche sympathizer! I'll be the latest idle gossip, because we all know that no one in this village ever shuts up. They just talk and talk and talk, especially Old Man Kranken,"

Ruby gasped. "Speaking of which, did you hear what he said about—"

"Actually Ruby, do you smell something?" Grey interrupted.

"You mean food? Seeing how we're in a tavern?" she asked with one eye brow raised and her arms crossed.

"No, something else." Grey pointed towards the kitchen, and under his breath, I heard him mumble something, but I couldn't make it quite out.

Smoke started entering the dining area from the kitchen. "Oh no! My chicken!" Ruby said in a panic.

"Transmedo!" She disappeared.

"Crap," I mumbled, still thinking about the locket. I lost it, and now it was in the hands of that bunter or their authorities. Hopefully, it would be a while before my parents would notice its disappearance.

"What's wrong?" asked Grey.

"It's—" I was about to mention the locket. However, I ultimately decided that maybe it would be best not to. "Nothing. It's nothing."

"If it's anything that Ruby said—"

"It's not." I rolled my eyes at the thought of Ruby's words. "Although, I wish that I wouldn't feel bad if her chicken burns, but I suppose it's a better alternative to punching her in the face."

"You'll do nothing," he warned.

"I wouldn't actually do that, but you heard everything that she just said. I'm not disgusting or idiotic. She at least deserves to be told off."

"Are you trying to end up dead? We're in a room filled with people that would kill you if they knew what you are."

"What I am?" I scoffed. "What exactly is that supposed to mean? I'm a person."

"Don't be so sensitive. You know what I mean."

"Do I? Why don't you explain it to me?"

"Why are you being so difficult?"

"Because you're an insensitive kidnapping asshole!" I stood up.

"Sit down!" he whispered.

"No! I'm going to go check to see if there are no more soldiers, so I can finally leave and go home." I shoved my chair back and turned to leave. I didn't realize that Ruby had teleported herself right behind me, and I nearly collided into her. She made direct eye contact with me, stunned. She had floating mugs of ale beside her that instantly fell and shattered on the ground. She did not move, so I took a step back.

"YOU?" she shouted.

The guests turned their heads and stared at us.

Grey stood up.

"We're leaving," he said.

"Claudere!" Ruby said. All of the doors and windows slammed shut. "You're not going anywhere!"

The music halted.

Ruby's eyes fixated on me.

"So, it is true? You're the one." Her eyes traveled over to Grey. "How could you? Harboring it?"

"I'm not an it!" I said.

"This is low even for you, Grey. Holding a fucking syche and bringing it here among us!"

Whispers arose.

"Knew something was off when they walked in."

"The only good syche is a dead syche."

"The old drunkard wasn't so crazy after all."

Everyone in the pub began to close in, encasing the three of us into a circle. I had never thought of myself as claustrophobic before, but as more and more sorcerers approached us, I became suddenly convinced that maybe I was now.

"You don't have to do this, Ruby," Grey said.

"You are either with the Crown or against the Crown, Grey. So, I suggest you pick a side," she said.

"Ruby, think about this. You literally just—" he began.

"Oh, well that was a favor," Ruby interrupted. She smiled, and her voice became disturbingly calm. "But this, this is treason. I like you, Grey, which is why I'll vouch for you. I will always vouch for you, and I am sure everyone here may even forgive you, provided that you do the right thing."

Ruby extended her hand towards him.

I looked over at Grey. My mind was racing.

Oh crap. Please, don't take her hand. Bare minimum, all of these sorcerers clearly want to hurt me. Shit, why did I stand up? I should have just listened for once. Grey, give me some assurance that you are still on my side!

Grey hesitated. He looked around at the crowd and then averted his eyes to the floor. He bit his bottom lip and touched his forehead with his hand. He sighed.

"Fine," he said.

"What?" I asked.

"Take her." He looked back up at Ruby. "You know that I can't afford anything else against the Crown."

I was near speechless. What was I hearing? He couldn't do this!

"You're right, I do," Ruby said.

"So, take her. Have her."

"NO!" I finally blurted out. "Grey, earlier you said—"

"You made the right choice, Grey," Ruby interrupted.

He grabbed his hooded caped and draped it over his shoulders.

"Grey," I said, softly, pleading for help.

He looked over in my direction, but he did not meet my eyes.

"I'm sorry, Cass. *Transmedo!*" Grey said.

"WAIT!" I yelled.

He vanished.

Oh no! I looked around at room full of devilish snared faces. My stomach twisted and I breathed slowly, attempting to calm the sound of my heart exploding through my chest and eardrums. I concentrated on every inch of my body to keep it from shaking.

"Detra Arma!" Multiple sorcerers fired blue, green, and gray blasts at me.

I waved my hands, levitating the chairs and table to swirl around me and block the spells. When they struck the furniture, some disintegrated, while others broke in half. I levitated more for cover. Soon, I would be out of furniture. *Plan B. Plan B. What's Plan B?*

There was only so much time in which I could keep this up. I looked up and noticed a hole in the ceiling. The hole was pitch black and I didn't know what was up there, but I knew that this may be my only shot.

I stretched my arms out, causing the remaining furniture to fly out towards all of the sorcerers. Some jumped, some scrambled, and others used spells to either block or destroy the chairs, tables, and dishes hurtling towards them. I jumped up into the air, using my gift to attempt to levitate myself towards the hole. I struggled, concentrating solely on reaching that part of the ceiling. Sweat emerged along the edges of my forehead, and my limbs trembled as I got closer.

I reached my hand out towards the hole. I was slim, and possibly able to fit through it. I was inching closer and closer towards it. My fingers nearly graced its surface when I felt a hot shock in my lower back.

"AHHH!" A wave of energy that felt like fire mixed with lightning passed through me. I struggled to keep my position in the air. My limbs became heavier, and my vision became static, as strength left my muscles. I kept shaking my head, trying to stay focused. I kept my hands outstretched towards the hole. I was almost there. I felt myself slipping until I could no longer hold myself up, and with a hard *thud,* I fell straight to the floor.

I landed on my side in the center of everyone, luckily not breaking any limbs. They swarmed closer, around me. My vision was quickly fading to nothing. I couldn't move.

Whispers arose, again.

"Is she dead?"

"What do we do with it?"

"Shouldn't we kill it?"

"Get ahold of yourselves." Ruby's voice broke through. "Do you want to be taken in for treason? We will do what we are instructed to do. Send word to His Majesty's court of its capture."

My heart continued to race. The petite tiny hairs on the back of my neck spiked up more, and goosebumps rose along nearly every inch of my skin. I longed for my parents. I longed to be with my sister. I longed to wake up, so I could be released from this nightmare.

The voices of the pub soon blended together and then faded, until I heard nothing.

WIC!

My head and back ached, and my knees were sore. Something cold, heavy, and metallic was weighing down all of my limbs. My hands were fully encased in that metal, and some sort of cloth that tasted like dirt was in my mouth. I opened my eyes.

Where am I?

I was bounded in chains inside of a large, enclosed wooden box. My tongue tried to push the cloth out of my mouth, but it would not move. The box itself, however, felt as if it were moving. It hit bumps and bounced me around. My eyes darted around the inside, until they stopped on a short and stubby man, sitting with an angry scowl upon his face. He held a long sword, and pointed it at me. "Don't try anything," he warned.

I sat there shaking, and my heart pounding a million times a minute. It didn't take long to realize that I was in a moving wagon. My heart finally slowed when the sorcerer let his guard down and slowly drifted off to sleep. I began to use telekinesis to rattle the structure that held my hands. I wanted to see if I could find a small crack or hole or anything in it that would allow my telekinesis to travel through it. There was nothing.

The road was uneven, and filled with cracks and holes, causing me to bounce up and down inside the wagon. The sorcerer woke up in a panic and grabbed his sword. When he saw that I was still tied up, he lowered it and closed his eyes.

I sat quietly, pondering and waiting for an idea on how to escape to come, but nothing came. I could not even get the chains off. I nearly shivered, and my eyes glistened at the unknown of what would happen to me next.

As the wagon continued to travel, a soft sound echoed from the ceiling. I looked up. The sound started on the other end of the box, but began to walk closer towards me. I tightened my chest and stopped breathing. The sound stopped in the middle of the ceiling. I took a deep breath, remembering to breathe again. A slim green light shone through the wooden ceiling and reached the floor. It traveled in the shape of a square, cutting the wood like a laser. When the shape was completed, the piece of wooden roof began to fall. However, mid fall it suddenly stopped. It flew back up into the air with the words,

"*Capara wood!*"

I knew that voice. *That bastard!*

The wood went through the square-shaped hole in the ceiling, and through it jumped Grey.

The sorcerer woke up from the noise of Grey's landing.

"What the—" he began.

Quickly, Grey turned to him while saying, *"Ad Somum!"*

A green light shot from his hands and into the sorcerer's head, whose eyes closed again, and he fell to his side, sound asleep.

"Huh, that was a lot easier than I thought." Grey looked back over at me, glaring at him. "I can explain, but let's get you out of here first."

He walked over to the unconscious sorcerer, bent down, and searched his person for something. I assumed a key. "Ah, come on. Chains like those always come with one," he said.

Eventually he found a petite, slender golden rod, with a half circle attached to the top of it. I stared at it, puzzled. What was that? He walked behind me, knelt down, and touched the chains with the tip of the half circle on the rod. Tiny orange and yellow sparks flew from the corner of my eye. Both the chains and metallic structure that held my hands unlocked themselves and fell to the floor. Grey threw the rod back over to the sleepy sorcerer. Before I pulled the gag out of my mouth, he grabbed my wrist and pulled me up. He said, "Let's go. *Transmedo!*"

We vanished.

We reappeared in the middle of a forest. My stomach felt uneasy from the teleporting, but I paid it no mind. My thoughts and emotions were elsewhere. I pulled the gag out of my mouth and pushed Grey away from me. "What the fuck was that!? You left me in that damn pub to die!"

"Cass—" he attempted.

"No! Don't call me that! That is not my name! My name is Alex, not Cass! I have every mind to give you something so much worse than another fuckin' black eye!"

"Oh, I'm sorry. I don't get a thank you for saving your life –again— when you were the one who blew our cover in the first place!" he said.

"A thank you!? You were an ass, and you left me for dead!"

"Really!? And you think that we had a chance fighting against that many people at once? We would have both been captured! This way I knew that I could break you out. Plus, I knew that they weren't going to kill you."

"How!? How could you possibly know that!?" I asked.

"Any spotted psychic is to be captured and taken to court for questioning. To kill you when you could have had useful information against your own people—"

"That's ridiculous! Look at me. Do I look like some spy or soldier or someone from the government? What information could I possible have?"

"They don't know that. You think that spies go around telling other people that they're spies instead of trying to blend in? Besides, its treason to act against the Crown's wishes."

I was still angry. I turned away and nearly tripped over the long skirt of the dress. "Damn it!"

I balled my fists and smacked them against the dress's skirt. "I still have to deal with this damn thing!"

I lifted the skirt up to prevent it from dragging. "Do you have a dagger or a knife or whatever else you wics ridiculously carry around?"

"What did you just call me?" Grey's tone quickly became sharp.

"Yeah, sucks when people call you that, doesn't it?" I remarked.

We both paused.

"Cass—" he began.

"I told you that's not my name," I interrupted.

"I was never going to just leave you without coming back." His tone had relaxed. "It was the only plan that I could think of, and I didn't have a way to tell you. I followed you and the wagon here. And Cass?"

"What?" I asked, still annoyed.

"I know that it's not your real name, but do you really want other sorcerers to know your real name?"

"I suppose not." I turned back around and faced him. Kind eyes and a half-smile laid upon his face. I believed him. But a small part of me felt like, despite all of his attempts to ask me to trust him, he had never even attempted to trust me.

He did take the chain off…again, but that shouldn't matter. He still did what he did at the pub. On the other hand, maybe I couldn't fault him for not trusting a stranger.

"I want you to start trusting me," I said.

"What?"

"Even if you had time to tell me your plan, I don't think that you would have trusted me enough to tell it to me. But, if I know what's going on, then maybe we can avoid some of this."

Grey pondered for a moment. "Okay. We can start now. Tell me what you want to do or wherever you want to go. I'll help you."

I stared at him silently, until I sighed and leaned my back against a tree trunk. I folded my arms. "Well, my parents are going to kill me. I have to go home. The only reason I was outside was to enjoy my last venture in the woods."

"Last?"

"Yup, my parents try to keep a very watchful eye on me, to say the least. I am so dead when I get home, and I doubt that I am ever going to see the light of day again, but even if I wanted to stay out here, I can't exactly do that, can I? Not with everyone trying to capture me."

"That's depressing."

"Well, you know."

"If I could just make a suggestion?"

"What?"

"Well, obviously we can't stay here, but I do know a safe place that we could go. There are going to be a lot of sorcerers, especially bunters, out looking for you near and around the border, since they know that's where you came from. If we go back there now, we'll definitely get captured. But, if we lay low for a little while, it will be a lot safer, and then I promise I will you get home," Grey said.

"Remind me why I should trust you, again?" I asked.

"Really? After all of that talk on why I should trust you?"

I held in my chuckle. "Fair."

"Besides, we really do need a safe place to stay for a little while so we can let all of this die down. The king—"

"The king? Wait, King Zentos?" I interrupted.

"Yeah. How did you...Huh, so you don't live under a rock as much as you let on?" he asked.

I knew very little about King Zentos, other than the fact that he was the sorcerer's monarch, and of course the one who initiated the war. The few times that I actually heard or saw my parents talk about him specifically, it was always in passing, and they would immediately become quiet if they saw me.

"Very funny, but I still can't imagine a king wanting anything to do with someone like me."

"Honestly, His Majesty," he began with such distain in his voice, "hates your kind a lot more than most of the people here, so while I don't know exactly what would have happened, I'm sure it's nothing good."

"But why? You are the ones that invaded us. If anything-"

"If anything what?" Grey's voice suddenly became very serious.

I was taken aback by his tone. Even his face had hardened. I slightly opened my mouth, but no sound came out.

Grey continued, "Listen, I was three when the war started. I don't really know or care about what happened. But I wouldn't go around saying lies like that."

"It's...it's not a lie." My parents wouldn't lie to me, especially about that. Dad was such an advocate for history. Grey had to be lying.

"It's a lie if the Crown says that it's a lie," he said.

"Do you trust the Crown?"

"It doesn't matter." Grey looked around the woods. "People have disappeared for saying less, unless you want that to happen."

Unsure of what to do or what to say, I did the only think I could think of. "Do you or do you not have that knife?"

"What?" he asked.

"A knife, a dagger or anything sharp," I said.

"Why?"

"Do you really expect me to be able to walk around in this?" I asked, gesturing to the round skirt.

He stared at me for a few seconds with a puzzled look across his face, until he finally relaxed it and reached into his pocket. He pulled out his woven sack. He reached inside it and pulled out a dagger.

"Here." Grey tossed it to me, and I caught it.

I began to cut the skirt of the dress a little past my knees. I jabbed the blade into the dress and dragged it across to tear. "Damn, this is thick," I mumbled.

I tightly gripped the handle and continued to crookedly cut the heavy fabric. "Better," I said.

"You know, you are definitely different," Grey said.

"So, what's that supposed to mean?"

"Hey, it's not a bad thing."

I motioned to toss him back his dagger, but he said, "No, keep it."

"Are you sure?"

"Yeah, it suits you. Besides, maybe with it you won't need as much rescuing," he teased.

"I will cut you."

"You sure about that?"

I walked up to him, his face inches away from mine. "Try me," I said.

"Scary part is that a part of me actually believes you." He smirked. Grey took a step back and aimed his palms towards my waist. *"Abere!"*

The dagger shot from my hand and latched itself onto the dress as if it were in a scabbard. I looked down at it and back at him.

"What?" he asked. "It's not exactly safe to be running around with a dagger in your hand."

I looked back down at the dagger. It stayed perfectly still. "Just like telekinesis," I mumbled.

Grey looked over my shoulder and stretched out his hand. *"Capara fabric!"*

The fallen fabric from the dress flew past me and into Grey's hand as a large clump. He pulled out his small sack from his pocket and dropped the fabric into the sack. My eyes widened. It still amazed me on how such a small bag could engulf items so much larger than it.

"Sorry. Forgot about that," I said.

"It's fine." He smirked. Grey turned and began to walk away. "Hey, are you coming or what?"

He stopped and gazed back at me.

"The next adventure awaits," he said.

"Just like the onion boy from the book," I whispered.

I let out a small grin, but hid it as I ran to catch up. "Yeah, well next time something happens, I come up with the plan. At this rate, you're going to get us both killed. Also, Grey?"

"Yeah?"

"I'm sorry about the black eye."

RICHARD STECKLAR

CERTAMEN AD MORTEM

Seven Days Later...
Dad and Mom each carried a bag strapped across their shoulder that stored their collapsed necessities of shelter, food, and tools. Holstered to their waists were extra weapons, hidden by their capes. Dad walked in front.

"Crap!" Mom mumbled.

He stopped and turned to face his wife.

She had gotten her foot stuck in a small patch of sinking mud. It was slower than quicksand, but still would grab a hold of anything that it could pull in. The mud was not rare, but it was scarce in these forests.

"Are you okay?" Dad asked.

She wiggled her foot.

"Hold on, let me—" he began.

"No, it's fine," Mom interrupted. Her tone was sharp, and her voice was quick.

Dad stopped. He folded his arms and patiently waited. Mom opened the palms of her hands and tilted them towards the mud. The body of the mud began to squish and swirl back and forth around her, gradually loosening its grip around her ankle and the sides of her foot. She let one hand remain in place, but directed it straight towards the ground. She stood calmly for a moment, then in one swoop, shot up into the air and fell backwards a few feet away, landing calmly on her feet.

"Even when not physically touching it, it still feels gross," Mom said, twiddling her fingers.

"I could have helped you," Dad said.

"I told you that it's fine." Mom smeared some of the mud residue off her boot and onto the ground.

"Why don't we take a break?" Dad suggested. He set his bag down.

"We've been walking—"

"No. It's already been a week, and we're losing daylight. According to the tracker, she is still travelling further in Perencia, so if you really want to take a break, then fine, take a break. I'm still going. It's up to you if you want to follow or not."

Mom walked forward, and just as she was about to pass Dad, he said, "We haven't talked about it yet."

She stopped.

"What is there to talk about?" she asked.

"Gabby."

"You mean how I told you that we should have told her?" She turned to face her husband. "That maybe if we did, then none of this would ever have happened? Or, let's see, I have another one. How living trapped underground was your idea!?"

She was just shy of shouting.

"You knew that I never liked that idea!" Mom said.

She lifted her hand up to her mouth as her head titled down towards the ground and the tears began to flow from her eyes.

"Gabby—" Dad reached his hand out towards Mom's shoulder, but she quickly pushed it away.

"We had no choice. It's not like we would have been safe with our kind either, you know that," he said.

His voice was neither stern, nor hard, nor angry. It was soft, soothing, and kind. He gently placed one hand on each of her shoulders. "Gabby, look at me."

She shook her head.

"Please," he said.

Slowly, she looked up at him.

"I know that there is nothing that I can say right now to make any of this better, but every choice or decision that I made was to protect Alex, to protect all of us. If I had known—" Dad sighed. He averted eyes and looked off to the side.

"He is ruthless. If he finds her—" Mom said.

"We've been hiding for fourteen years." Dad looked back at Mom. "Even if he gets alerted, he won't know her exact location, especially with her having no magic to track."

"But her pattern. She is obviously travelling with at least one other person, clearly one of them. If they find out or try to lead her into a trap…" Mom's voice began to shake.

"She would either be dead or would have been taken to the castle by now, if that was the case," Dad said.

"I can't go through it again."

Dad wrapped his arms around his wife, pulling her in as she pressed her head against his chest. She wrapped her arms around him and dropped her bag.

"I know," he whispered. "We just have to have faith that for now she will be okay."

"Richard?"

"Yes?"

"I'm still mad at you."

"I know, but—" he stopped. His grip around Mom tightened, and he pulled her in closer.

"You don't really think this is the time to—" Mom began.

He leaned in and whispered something in her ear. She continued to hug him, but freed her fingers. She extended them out, and gently and subtly moved them up and down one by one in the air.

"There," she giggled.

Her hands went straight as her fingers collapsed into each other. Her right hand let go of my father, and sharply cut through the air, creating a concentrated wind of telekinetic force. She spun around from my father and held both of her hands up, as if she were holding an invisible rope. She pulled her hands towards her, and through the leaves, bushes, and corners of the trees came a brown-hooded sorcerer flying towards them. When he was only a few feet away, Mom spread out her hands and flattened them. Telekinetically, she caused him to fall forward onto his stomach, and froze his movements.

"Who are you, and what do you want?" she asked.

The sorcerer only groaned.

Dad walked up to him and bent down at his side.

"Where are they? We already know that there are more," Dad said.

"Fuckin' syche!" The sorcerer spat at Dad.

"So be it." Dad motioned his hand towards the sorcerer, but then stopped. He heard whispers. Dad looked back at Mom. "Gabby, duck!"

Mom jumped down to the ground as a blue spell came hurtling

from behind. Simultaneously, Dad pressed a button on his communicator watch, creating a boxed shield to face the spell. The sorcerer began to stand back up. As he started to whisper, Dad turned and grabbed the small electric taser from his holster. The taser shot electrical currents from its conductors into the sorcerer. The sorcerer's entire body shook before he fell backwards onto ground. The hood on his head fell back, revealing his boiled flesh as smoke arose from it like melted butter on a frying pan. His short, brown hair was charred in spikes. His blue eyes were still open. And his body laid there, lifeless.

The spell collided into Dad's shield, creating sparks and making it hot. It continuously tried to push him back. He stood his ground, although not without a few struggles. The spell, unable to penetrate the shield, split in two. One flew to the right and the other to the left, blackening the tree trucks that they had consequently struck.

The forest was quiet.

Dad slipped the taser back into his holster, and Mom stood back up. She closed her eyes and gently moved her fingers through the air, using her gift to feel out the surroundings. She stopped and turned to her side. Palm facing out, she jabbed her hand out.

Another hooded sorcerer appeared out of nowhere. He fell backwards onto his back.

Crack! Crunch! Crack!

He laid there, seemingly immobile. Mom narrowed her eyes down on his body, with her palm still out.

"Wait!" she said.

The sorcerer's body began to slowly disappear and evaporate into the air.

More whispers.

"Gabby!" Dad looked back at Mom. He continued telepathically, "To your left, now!"

Mom quickly turned her upper body at her waist, while lifting a petite knife from her holster. She lifted her left arm and angled her elbow, jabbing it into the air.

"Ugh!!!!"

She twisted towards the groan and, with a knife, she quickly sliced through the air. Blood sprayed from the air and onto her hand and fingers. Another sorcerer appeared, seemingly the same figure that had just evaporated. His throat was gashed open, and his hands went to his neck as he desperately gasped for air. His body twitched, and blood drained down his neck and onto his burlap clothes.

Mom took a few steps back. She still held the knife, firmly in hand. She used her gift to wipe the blood off both her knife and hand.

The sorcerer fell to the ground. His twitching slowed, until it eventually stopped, along with his breathing. His blue eyes clouded, and his head fell slightly to the side. Blood continued to flow from his throat, coating both himself and the dirt beneath him red.

Two more sorcerers appeared. Their invisibility fell off like a veil. They stood beside each other. Instead of stricken by fear, they looked quite impressed. The one to the right was thin, tall, and had long, tangled brown hair placed back into a ponytail. His eyes were green, and accompanied by a tiny, mischievous smirk.

The other had light gray eyes and short blonde hair. He was shorter than his companion, yet still tall. He was also huskier and more muscular than his comrade. All of their clothing was of a simple brown, burlap cloth.

Both sorcerers looked over at their fallen companions.

"Pity," said the brunette. He took a step forward.

Mom pointed her hands towards him.

"Don't move. What do you want?" she asked.

"My fair lady." The brunette politely gestured with his hands. "Who said that we wanted anything?"

"And is that why you were planning on attacking us?" she asked.

"Hmm," he pointed at her. "Clearly, you are the telekinetic one. So, he—" the brunette looked over at Dad, "must be the telepathic one."

He snickered.

Dad walked up next to Mom.

"Makes sense. Of course, we were planning on if seeing either of you had any valuable possessions that we could so kindly take off your hands. Not always, but every so often, you find a traveler with something special. Maybe an enchanted trinket or an orb of some sort, so many different kinds of those nowadays. So imagine our surprise that when I pulled out my wand, and it sensed no magical energy, neither around you nor inside you. You'll have to pardon me, when I beg the question." Although at first lighthearted and playful, his voice shifted to a harsher tone when he asked, "What are two lone syches like yourselves doing in these woods?"

"If you ask me, I think the price of the heads of two syches for His Majesty would be worth far more gold than any trinket or orb. Wouldn't you say?"

"We are only mere travelers, who have nothing to do with any conflict or war. Walk away now, and we can all pretend like this never happened," Dad said.

"Travelers?" the brunette scoffed. He crossed his arms and raised one eyebrow. "With talents such as yours? Tell me, does that line normally work?"

"Everyone knows how to fight in times such as these."

"And?"

"Okay." Dad's tone dropped, and his eyes narrowed into the brunette's green eyes. "New, negotiation. We easily took out both of your wic friends. What makes you think that you will be able to kill us so easily?"

The brunette lifted up his nose in a scowl. He held it there, while still staring at my father. A few seconds passed until he allowed his face to relax into a mischievous smile.

"Oh yes, they were weak, weren't they? Terrible recruits, mere amateurs really. But you two." He openly gestured with both hands, and his voice became lighthearted once again. Dad saw a gleam of delight in his eyes. The sorcerer's face relaxed into a large grin. "Well, this should be most interesting. A fun sport. Our own *certamen ad mortem*. So, what do you say?"

"Fine," Dad said.

The brunette placed his right hand on his chest over his heart and gracefully extended his left arm out to his side. He bent his knees and leaned his upper body slightly forward in a light bow. His partner did not bend his knees, though he did place his right hand over his heart and give a nod over to his opponents.

They returned the gesture with a nod.

The brunette stood back up, straightening his posture. His face gleamed with delight from his iniquitous smile. He motioned his hands together. They were cupped, facing each other without the hands actually touching.

"Praclarus!" said the brunette. A petite, bright green flame appeared in the space between his hands, making the inside of them glow.

Mom fell into her fighting stance. Dad, however, slipped his fingers to the holster around his waist and pulled out a small metal cylinder that was barely the size of his hand. He squeezed it, and it expanded into a long six-foot bow staff with razor-sharp barbs on each end.

"Shall we begin?" asked the brunette.

And his companion quickly followed suit.

ALEXANDRIA

MY LADY

Grey stood, barefoot with of both his sleeves' and pants' legs rolled up in the shallow end of a brown river. I watched him as he stood perfectly still. He was hunched over, with his hands in front of him, ready to pounce. He eyed his oncoming prey. It gently swam towards him, accompanied by the soft and gentle current. Right before it approached his feet, his hands lunged at the fish. "Finally!" he exclaimed.

He picked the fish up out of the water. It wiggled and squirmed aggressively until it escaped until it his grasp and fell back into the water. "So close!"

I hid my chuckle behind my hands. For one so accustomed to travelling and camping out in woods, you would think that he would be a little better at fishing. Yet, he...I mean, it was kind of charming. My mouth relaxed into a soft smile. He always caught one eventually, though.

I turned from Grey. I was sitting on a log by a campfire as the sun began to set. The fire's orange and yellow flames popped, and its wood-burning scent rose into the air before being disbursed throughout our settled area by a light wind. It mixed in with the natural musk of the plants, fish, and minerals from the river. The sky was different layers of pink, yellow, and blue, with only a few clouds in the sky. It was perfect. I turned my head, looking back at Grey. "Need some help there?"

"No, it's okay. I got this," he said.

"You sure?"

"Yes, you got lucky last time."

"Yeah, sure," I mumbled as I rolled my eyes, but secretly I was happy to not have to get up.

We had been walking for a week through the forests, and it was good to finally sit and take a break. I closed my eyes, and in the distance I began to hear a quick-paced tune. Its melody was joyful, and soon it was accompanied by the faint sounds of cheers. In a strange way, it actually blended quite well with the chatter of the forest, complimenting the tunes of the crickets and frogs that sung along the stream and throughout the forest. It was like a special concert, made just for us to enjoy.

According to Grey, there was another town nearby. I opened my eyes. Rising into sky were multiple paper lanterns that glowed like oversized lightning bugs in hues of red, yellow, purple, and green. "They're so pretty."

The lights of the lanterns bled into the sky. It was getting darker, and I was becoming mesmerized by the growing contrast of light and dark.

"Got one!" Grey said.

The lanterns were of different shapes and sizes. Some were square. Others were oval, while others were large or small stars. My hand reached out towards the sky, as if I could touch one of the lanterns, until I saw one in the shape of a heart.

My breath halted, and I retracted my hand. Flashes of the silver heart-shaped locket entered my mind. I saw its chain, and the swirls along its body.

The Locket. The voice of the locket echoed in my ears. Its silver swirls shined, vibrantly in my memory. I looked over to my right, to my left, and then down at the ground. There were only trees, bushes, dirt, and grass.

It was only me. It was only just in my head.

I sighed, not sure if I was feeling relief or grief. On one hand, the locket made me feel crazy, hearing that voice in my head. On the other hand, I still lost a piece of jewelry that belonged to my parents. I had no idea how valuable it was.

No. I didn't want to think about it. I refused to think about it. I shook the image of the locket out of my head.

"Cass…CASS!?"

"What?" I jumped. I opened my eyes and gripped the bark of the log. I planted my feet firmly on the ground to prevent myself from falling. I turned back towards Grey.

"I caught one!" He proudly held up a large fish. It squirmed in his hands.

"Oh, great." I turned back around.

"For someone who loves food so much, you would think that she would at least be a little excited."

The rocking sound of the fish dropping into the tin bucket dispersed into the air. It was then replaced by the growing sound of the crunching grass beneath Grey's feet.

"What are you looking at?" Grey was now right behind me.

I pointed up. Although the heart-shaped lantern gave me chills, the rest of the lanterns were still beautiful.

"The lanterns. There must be a festival or something going on."

He set the bucket on the ground and sat down beside me. "I take it there's not too many festivals where you're from?" he asked.

"No, not when you live in the middle of nowhere and your parents don't let you out."

"They really didn't let you go anywhere?"

"No." I shook my head. "They're very strict, but my mom once told me about the parties and celebrations that she went to when they were younger, and I've read about them. The dancing. The music. Actually, getting the chance to pleasantly be around other people."

"So, what did you and your family do for fun?" he asked.

"Nothing," I said and snickered at the same time.

"Nothing?"

"Well, I read. My mom and my sister draw, and my dad is really into tech stuff. He also likes to read."

"That's it? Nothing else? No friends? Or neighbors?"

I shook my head. "No. That was all before the war. My family went into hiding, and literally all of my memories are of our home. It's just us."

There was a slight pause, only filled with the popping of the fire.

I continued, "But, when my sister and I were little, we played and invented our own imaginary scenarios. Mine always had dragons and winged horses. They were just couch cushions or a broom or something like that."

I smiled.

"Wow," Grey said.

"What?"

"Your life sucks."

"And, you're such an ass." Although as much as I tried, I couldn't keep a straight face. The laughter seeped through my lips and I gently shoved his shoulder.

He laughed too.

"Ey, not my fault. But I am a little surprised that your imaginary battles were with magical creatures. Figured such things would be banned from a psychic home."

"My parents don't hate magic. They just don't trust it, or sorcerers, or really anyone. Come to think of it, it's actually kinda weird. Also, in my defense, the dragons were always evil, and my sister and I always defeated them, so of course the psychics always won."

"Well, rest assured a lot of those magical creatures have long gone extinct, except for pixies. They're really rare now."

"I know. It was all in my books."

"Wow, even magical books."

"I know, the irony. I'm not sure where it was, but I think the closest town to us was a sorcerer town where my parents would get little treats and goodies once in awhile, along with art supplies, and at times a new book, especially on my birthday. Of course, we still had our books on technology and history and other things. But one, history is boring and two, I've read a lot of the books that we own like a million times anyway, so it was always nice to get something new. Plus, my dad is such an intellectual that I think he is just happy that I found an interest in reading, whatever it was," I said.

"Fair enough." He chuckled. "Gotta' favorite?"

"The Knight Chronicles: The Stag Versus the Lion."

"So, you're also a knight?" Grey teased.

"Shut up. Ha-ha. It's a great story that allowed me to escape my gray walls and out into a land of adventure."

"Well," Grey stood up, "let's say we detour from this adventure and take a new one, a short one."

"What are you talking about?" I asked.

"You just said that you've never been to a party, right?"

I chuckled. "What? Are you insane? I thought you said earlier that you didn't want anyone to see us. We can't go to a party."

"I'm not saying that we should go into the village, but that doesn't mean that we can't have our own. There is music and lights." He looked and pointed up towards the lanterns. And then his eyes came back down towards me. "And people."

"You're insane." I chuckled, again.

"Come on," Grey extended his hand towards me.

Nervously I asked, "What are you doing?"

"Embarking on another adventure."

I looked at him, confused with one eyebrow raised.

He chuckled. "Dancing, only dancing."

"Oh, but I um...I don't know how."

"So? Who cares? It's not like anyone's here to judge."

I took his hand and stood up. Grey stood in front of me and asked, "Ready?"

I laughed. "No."

"You'll be fine."

Grey gently pulled me forward with one hand, and he placed his other hand gently against my shoulder blade on my back. I fastened my lips shut, and my breath froze inside of me. It suddenly dawned me that I had never been this close to a boy before. I gazed up at his face. He smiled. I smiled. I realized that I liked being this close to him.

Grey pulled me closer, but I stepped too far and landed on his foot.

"Sorry," I said.

"It's okay," Grey said. We both stepped to the side, his left and my right still in contact, and then I stepped on it again.

"Sorry. See, I'm horrible at this," I said, still giggling.

Grey chuckled. "It's fine. Don't worry about it. You just need practice."

I stepped without stepping on his foot.

"See, there ya go," Grey said.

"Uh huh, I'm a real expert now," I said, sarcastically.

"Well, Expert, what do you say we take this up a notch?"

"Uh oh."

"What? Why, uh oh?"

I laughed. "Nothing."

"Alright. Ready. Set. Go!" Grey said.

He pulled me in closer, and started dancing faster and faster, carrying me along with him. We jumped around the campsite in a circle.

Our laughter grew, especially when I lost my footing and almost fell. Grey caught me, still holding me in his arms.

"Oops, maybe that was a little too fast. Are you alright?" he asked.

"Yeah, I'm okay."

As I stood back up, the music began to slow. The beat changed from upbeat and fast to a slower mid-tempo. Grey took a step back. He bowed and said, "My Lady."

I chuckled. "Stop. You're ridiculous."

He stood up straight and extended his hand, once again. I took it and we danced.

You would think that a slower dance would have been easier, but it seemed to be that much harder. I found myself stepping on his feet even more. "Sorry," I kept saying.

I gazed down at my feet. I sighed in relief that they were finally not colliding into his.

"Don't look down," he said.

"I keep messing up. I'm sure that you don't want me to keep stepping on you."

"It's okay. It's just that you're not supposed to look down. You're only supposed to look at your partner. Let me lead you, and you won't step on my feet."

I looked up at his face. It was warm and with a happy grin across it. It made me grin, as well.

Grey continued, "Don't move until I do, and just put a little more tension in this hand."

He gently squeezed my right hand, the hand that he held.

I did.

"Yeah, just like that. So when I push like this," and he did, "you feel it and take a step back. And when I don't push or pull, you don't anticipate anything, and—"

"Keep stepping on your feet?" I asked.

"Well, I wasn't going to say that, but—"

We both laughed.

"The same also goes for when we go to the side. Just don't break the frame, which is the shape and tension in our arms and hand. It will be a lot hard to feel what I'm about to do if you. Let's try." We went to the side. "Yeah, just like that. One, two, three. One, two, three. One, two, three."

"What?" I questioned.

"Nothing, it's supposed to help. It's something that my mother drilled into me when she taught me."

"Your mom? You've never mentioned her before."

"Oh yeah, dancing was her favorite hobby, so of course I was forced into it. I hated every minute of it then, but I don't think that it's so bad now."

"Does she still dance?"

"She can't. She's dead."

"Oh, Grey. I'm so sorry. I didn't know."

"It's okay. It doesn't matter. It was a long time ago," he said in reassurance.

Grey smiled. He lifted up his hand, and gently guided me forward into a twirl with his other hand. I giggled.

"Does your dad like to dance?" I asked.

"I don't know. He died when I was baby."

"Oh, crap." I stopped. "I'm so sorry. I um, crap." I wasn't sure what to say. I was afraid that I was going to say something else that would make it worse.

"I promise, it's fine," Grey said.

He re-extended his hand. I took it, but we remained quiet while dancing, until he finally broke the silence. "I'm not going to lie, it does suck. But I never knew him anyway, and you can't change the past."

"Do you ever think about it? Or about your mom?" I asked.

He hardened his expression.

"I prefer not to. Like I said, you can't change the past."

Although there wasn't much change in his tone, it was quite obvious that this was not a subject that he wished to talk about.

The music became even slower, evolving into a softer and more soothing beat.

"The music changed," I said, awkwardly.

"Yeah, it did."

Grey leaned in my ear and whispered, "Do you want to know a secret?"

"Uh, sure," I said.

"Okay. You..." he began.

What was he going to say? My heart was beating, and I wondered if he could feel it.

He continued: "…are a terrible dancer."

"Oh, you are the worst!" I pushed him away, while trying to hold back the laughter in my voice.

He, on the other hand, did not hold back any of his laughter. He smiled, with his emerald eyes shining. Suddenly, my palms were warm. Grey re-extended his hand, and I took it. Gently, he guided me to come in closer, and placed his other hand back on my shoulder blade. My stomach fluttered.

"Is this okay?" he asked.

I felt my cheeks become red.

"Yeah, why wouldn't it be? It's just dancing, right?" Even my voice was starting to sound weird. It was slightly higher pitched than normal.

What's wrong with me?

"Hey, Grey—" I began.

"Yeah?"

"Do you want to know a secret?"

"Sure, what's going on?" he asked.

"Okay." I lowered my voice, leaned in closer, and whispered: "You're a terrible lead."

"What?"

I took a few steps back and wrapped my arms around my stomach, attempting to contain my uncontrollable laughter.

"And you called me the worst." He smiled.

"Well."

"Well, what?" he asked.

I stepped up to him, as close as we were as when we were dancing slow. His emerald eyes peered into my golden eyes. I couldn't resist it any longer. I stuck my tongue out and made the raspberry sound by blowing air through my mouth into his face, and then quickly ran away.

"Hey, you little—" he said as he chased after me.

I circled the campsite with him close on my tail, until I eventually let him catch me. The floating lanterns and the music remained in the sky until late into the night. It felt good, for the first time, to be in the midst of my own adventure.

HANNAH

ALEX, WHERE ARE YOU?

Hannah laid on her bed in her black shorts and a large navy oversized t-shirt. Her eyes lingered on the ceiling, covered in the mixture of artistic yellow stars and misshapen ones. She stared in silence, until her nose scrunched and her eyes wept. She turned over onto her side and buried her face into the neatly-tucked blanket.

She was nearly asleep when her watch went off.

"HANNAH!"

She sat up in the bed. It was Mom, but her voice came from the watch.

"Mom? Dad? Where are you? Have you found Alex? Are you coming back?" The questions quickly oozed out from her lips.

"Sweetheart... lost Alex's signal."

"What—" Hannah began.

Mom's voice was intertwined with static. "...Urgent!" Her tone was stern. "We need you...access... father's laptop, now! I... you the password once...have it. It's in our bedroom in... black box underneath... bed."

Hannah hopped onto the floor. She grabbed the silver bow staff that Dad had given her from off the floor and, then ran out of the room.

Hannah sat at the kitchen counter with a silver laptop in front of her and the bow staff leaned against the counter. Her eyes darted back and forth across the screen, never breaking eye contact. Her hair was pulled back into a messy bun on top of her head, with a couple of strands that fell to the sides of her face.

"Can...hear me?"

"Barely," Hannah said. "You never explained what happened to your equipment?"

"It...damaged during a small encounter...fine...did... find the signal?"

"Not yet. But you never even explained what happened. Are you and Dad at least any closer to finding Alex? When are you all coming home?"

"Don't worry. We're...trail...everything...okay?"

"Sure," Hannah said, weakly. She clenched her jaw, keeping in her emotions. "Everything is fine."

"Good. I'm happy to hear that you are being strong. I promise... explain everything...get back. The impor....is getting your sister back."

"Where's Dad?" Hannah asked.

"Trying...fix...equipment. He's fine."

"Well," Hannah began.

Suddenly, the laptop started violently beeping. Hannah looked back at the screen and saw a red dot flashing on a digital map. She used the mouse of the computer to narrow in on the dot. As she zeroed in on the dot, the longitude and latitude numbers of the ground started to appear and narrow in on the screen.

"Hannah? Are you there?"

Hannah clicked 'Enter' on the laptop.

"Ahhhh!" she screamed. She stretched her arms out in the air and smiled.

"Han...uts wrong!?"

"I have a radius! Hold on, just give me a few minutes."

"...you sure?"

"Yes, quick! What's the tracker ISB number? I should be able to either re-establish the signal or connect it with mine once I have it."

"Emailing it to you with...watch now."

RICHARD STECKLAR

FOUND

Mom was sitting on the ground, typing the number "10081949" into her watch. She had a long thin cut along her right cheek, and patches of scratches and burns around her wrists and hands.

"And send," Mom said.

"How did it go?"

She nearly jumped. Mom looked behind her and saw Dad. He stood calmly, with his left forearm freshly bandaged.

"How long were you standing there?"

"Not long."

"Well." She stood up and turned around to face Dad. "She found a signal, and I just emailed her the code number. How's your arm?"

Mom reached out to touch it.

"The blood finally started clotting," Dad said.

"That's good. That blonde slashed you deep. Thankfully, it won't be any permanent damage. But are you sure that you're okay? You know how you like to pretend that everything is alright when it's not, especially when you get hurt," Mom said.

"That was one mission."

"More like five."

"Ha." Dad chuckled. "The good old days, huh? Although, everything considered..." he looked down at his arm, "...I probably deserved it."

"Probably."

"I'm still in the doghouse, I see."

"Well, no...at least not completely. I agreed to it. You didn't act on it alone. We were young when we had Hannah and then Alex." Mom sighed.

She continued: "Going into hiding seemed like the only option. You were right to have to us do it. I'm sorry I reacted the way that I did. I don't know what else we could have done."

Mom looked off to the side, trapped within her own thoughts.

"Gabby?"

Mom weakly smiled. "Do you miss it?" she asked.

"Of course. I'll never forget the honor of completing a mission," Dad said.

"And the celebration feasts! What I wouldn't give to have meals like that again, tortes and tarts galore."

"We would have had to retire, eventually."

Mom sighed and said, "I know." She faced Dad. "I don't regret it. Not any of it."

Dad stepped forward towards Mom and kissed her on her forehead. She wrapped her arms around him, and he wrapped his around hers, and they hugged each other. "We'll find her and bring her back home, safely," he said.

"I know. I'm just afraid of it happening again."

"It won't."

Mom took a deep breath.

Dad continued, "I don't know if this is a good time to ask, but how are your hands?"

"They'll heal. I wanted a break from the burn solution and bandages before I re-bandaged them again. But don't worry, I'm not going to leave them out for too long and let them get infected."

"MOM!"

They both jumped as Hannah's voice echoed from the watch. They let go of each other. Mom leaned forward and began to speak into the watch.

"Sweetheart, what is it!?" she asked.

"I found her! I'm sending you the signal now!" Hannah said.

The watch started to beep. Mom pressed one of the tiny buttons on the watch. "Her location's locked again! Good job, Hannah. You are my angel!" Mom said.

She jumped with excitement, and smiled at her husband. He softly returned the smile and held out his hand. She took off the watch and placed it in his palm.

Dad placed the watch around his wrist and held it up to his mouth.

"Lock target as destination."

"Destination set," said the watch.

"Are you ready?" he asked Mom.

"Always. Let's get our little girl," Mom said.

Dad put his arm around his wife. She leaned into his shoulder and looked up at his face, still grinning. He smiled back and said, "We're going to get her. Let's hurry and pack up."

ALEXANDRIA

THE LAKE

It was a few more days until we reached the outskirts of another tiny village, Silva Nux.

The sun had already set, and the sky was dark. I wore Grey's hooded cape in order to hide from the prick of the cool air, although I felt bad for having it. Grey was in a long-sleeved shirt that wasn't quite thick enough. I could tell that he was starting to get cold, even if he did not want to admit it. The night was colder than others, as if it was warning us that soon it would be time for snow. It was the first night in which we could see our breaths when we spoke. And the first night that I had secretly desired a hat to protect the inside of my ears from the chilly wind. How could he not be cold? Still, he kept insisting that I take the cape, and that he was fine.

We walked and walked, passing small homes on acres and acres of land, until we reached the last tiny house on the dirt road. It was the last plot of land that remained cleared before it turned back into forest. The house was an off-white, faded cottage with a dark brown wooden roof. It was only one story, and had a chimney with smoke rising from it. The front of the cottage was encased by a rectangular oak porch with wooden bars that came up to my waist.

I smiled.

My eyes shifted and widened at the sight of the large barn that towered over the cottage, even though it was still yards away. It was two stories high and darkened by the night, hardly differentiating itself from a shadow. There were bales of hay in front of its two large doors. The hay was bound, and the doors were closed.

"It's not much, but it's home sweet home," Grey said.

"It's perfect."

"Wow, well if you're impressed with this, I will have to show you the crops and the chicken coop behind the barn when there's more light." He smirked.

"Really!?" Excitement oozed out of my voice.

"Sure?" Grey said.

I had never seen a cottage before, or been on a farm. I had only seen pictures, and had read about them in books. Grey seemed puzzled at my amazement, but I was in awe of something new.

We walked onto the porch. It was a foot or two off the ground, aided by a few steps, and lit by a floating yellow lantern that hovered next to the front door. Unlike the decorative lanterns we saw in the woods, this one was made of glass, and held a small white candle burning inside of it.

Grey hovered his hand over the latch of the door. *"Adrae!"*

The latch of the door unlocked itself.

"That was a different spell than you used when we snuck into the barn at the tavern," I said.

"Different password," Grey said.

We stepped inside.

The air was warm and filled with the scent of tomatoes, spices, and bread. My stomach vibrated and growled, realizing how hungry it was. I looked up to see if Grey had heard it. His attentions seemed elsewhere.

Straight ahead was the kitchen. It had white walls outfitted with hickory and oak cabinets. Below them was a straight row of black iron pans hanging by their handles. The kitchen was mostly open. Its only a barrier was a countertop with streaks of different colored wood that stopped only about three feet away from the wall. A large black box sat next to a stone fireplace against the wall at the far end of the kitchen. It had two elegant little doors, like the doors of a manor, on its front, and there was a large silver pot with a lid on top of it. It faced a large horizontal white box with one large door.

To the left was the living area. Like the kitchen, the walls were white. There was an old sofa, stitched with different colored patches on its cushions and arms. It was accompanied by a table and three wooden chairs. Neither of them matched nor were the same stained colored wood. Up midway and to the right was another hallway that led to three small bedrooms and a bathroom.

"Alve, I thought that you wouldn't be back 'til tomorrow. How was the—?" Another voice spoke, and another teen boy stepped forth from the hall.

He saw us and jumped.

He was very tall, easily over six feet. His frame was long and thin. He had bright blue eyes accompanied by straight, almond-colored hair that fell nearly over his eyes in the front and to the bottom of his jawline along the sides and in the back. He wore similar clothes to Grey. He looked startled, with raised eyebrows, especially when he looked over at me and then back at Grey.

"Just me. Johnny, this is Cass," Grey said.

"Hi," I said, softy.

"I thought that you were Bradin," Johnny said.

"Clearly. Where is he?" Grey asked.

"He left for the Lopidus a few days ago. So, who's your friend?" Johnny pointed at me.

I looked from him to Grey, who in contrast was keeping his composure very relaxed. Was coming here a mistake like in the tavern? *Rawr!* My stomach growled again. This time I could feel the sting of my hunger slowly broiling in my stomach. I placed my hands against it.

"Yeah, sorry it's so late," Grey said.

"Yeah." It took a moment for Johnny to say another word, but he finally turned back to me and asked, "You hungry?"

"Yes!" I perked up.

"I made a pot of stew earlier. It's on the stove in the kitchen." He pointed at the black box behind him in the kitchen. "Feel free to help yourself."

"Thanks," I said.

As Grey and I took a few steps forward Johnny grabbed Grey's shoulder and asked, "Hey, can I talk to you for a second?"

"Uh, sure," Grey said.

I looked over at Grey. He smiled and said, "Start without me. I'll be quick."

"Okay," I said.

While I walked to the kitchen, Grey and Johnny walked into the hall.

Grey came back about fifteen minutes later. He walked up to me in the kitchen. I had already found a bowl and spoon, and was currently eating the stew.

"Sorry about that. Any good?" Grey asked.

I nodded, yes. "There are even actual chunks of tomatoes in it. I think that he's even got you beat," I teased.

"Johnny has always had a knack for cooking," Grey said.

"So, who exactly is Johnny?" I asked.

"The brother that I never had."

"And Bradin? He mentioned someone named Bradin."

"The older brother that I never had. Johnny's actual brother, though." Grey's tone seemed less chipper, as though he was less sure of himself.

"Is everything okay?" I asked.

"Yeah." Grey turned and grabbed another bowl and spoon. As he poured the stew into his bowl, he said, "You can sleep in my room tonight. I will take the couch in the living room."

"Thanks," I said.

A few drops of the broth began to trickle down the corner of my mouth. I turned to wipe my mouth and my chin with the back of my hand, only to turn back and see Grey grinning and shaking his head.

"What?" I asked.

"Nothing," he said.

The door opened, and the floor boards creaked.

"Cass. Cass, wake up!" Grey nudged my shoulder.

"What do you have against sleep?" I groaned. Despite the morning, I still remained in bed. I turned over and pulled the blue blanket that laid on top of me over my head.

"Hey, I want to show you something," Grey said.

"Come back later," I mumbled.

"*Capara plate!* Not even for this?" He lifted the blanket up with one hand and held a fork and a plate of toast and fried eggs with the other. "I know how much you like food."

I reached for the plate, but he pulled it away. "Are you going to get up?" he asked.

"Ugh, you're literally the worst. Fine," I said.

I sat up and stretched out my arms. Grey handed me the plate and fork. I grabbed it and began chowing down.

"Whoa there, pixie" Grey said. He chuckled, and I just rolled my eyes.

"But, there is something that I do want to show you," he said.

"What is it?" I asked.

"You'll see."

After I finished eating, Grey took the plate and rushed us out of the cottage. Johnny was already outside, carrying a large crate towards the barn. He looked over his shoulder and yelled, "Have fun!" as we ran.

Grey led me into the woods. He held my hand and guided me over fallen logs and long sweeping tree branches. "Where are we going?" I asked.

"Just a little further," he said.

We walked past another small stretch of trees, until we stopped. Grey opened a curtain of hanging leaves and vines from the trees. My eyes widened as I gazed upon the horizon. There were pastures of green with wild yellow and purple flowers surrounding a tiny wooden dock and a small lake that glistened in the sun.

"So, what do you think?" Grey asked.

"It's gorgeous!"

"Well, come on." He tugged my hand and we ran towards the dock.

When we reached the shore, Grey took his shirt off. He had abs. I found myself staring at them. His stomach was slender and toned, and his abs were so lean! My mind went slightly blank.

"Are you ready?" Grey asked.

"What?" I asked, snapping back to reality.

"To get in?"

"Oh, yeah. Water. That's right. We're um, yeah."

"Are you okay?" He raised one eyebrow.

"Yup." I gazed over at the water and suddenly became overcome with uneasiness at the pit of my stomach.

"What's wrong?" Grey asked.

"What?" I bit the bottom of my lip as my heart started to pound. "Nothing."

He looked back at the water, and then at me. "If you don't like swimming—" he began.

"No, it's not that," I interrupted. "Or, at least I don't know if I like it or not. I just um, that looks like a lot of water, like it could be really deep water."

"You don't know how to swim?"

"Well, as you can imagine, I've never really had the opportunity to learn or been anywhere near any body of water like this before."

"Did not think of that, but that's okay. I'll teach you."

"That's okay. Maybe I should just go back." I turned to walk away.

"Manera!" he said.

My feet were stuck to the ground, and I could not move them. "Grey," I said.

"Don't you want to at least try?"

I looked back at him over my shoulder.

"Fine. *Dimitas!"* He said.

I quickly, yet quietly waved my hand. I lifted up about a bucket's fill of water and threw it at Grey, hitting him from the back.

"Very funny," he said.

I turned back around. His hair and shoulders were soaking wet.

"I thought so," I said.

"You know, a few nights ago when we danced, you didn't want to at first, but you have to admit it turned out to be a fun adventure. You told me that your parents keep you locked up at home, so why not finally experience the things that you've read about in your books?" Grey asked.

He extended his hand.

I stood still, staring down at it.

"I mean, what do you have to lose?"

"Drowning is a little different than dancing."

"I won't let you drown. Trust me." He smiled.

I held in my sigh and took his hand.

"Transmedo!" He said, and we vanished.

As we reappeared on the dock, I held onto him to keep my balance. I was finally starting to get used to the teleporting, but I wasn't exactly used to the landing.

"Show off," I said.

"Always." He grinned.

Grey held out his palms towards the water and said, *"Cali!"*

A ring of green light appeared down in the water in front of us, then disappeared.

"Now your clothes won't get wet," he said. Grey took my hand and stood right next to me. "Are you ready?"

"No," I said, shaking my head and looking down at the water.

"I won't let you drown, I promise."

"You better not." I looked up at him. "Because then I'll just have to come back to life to kill you myself."

Grey chuckled. "I would expect nothing less, My Lady."

My cheeks turned red.

Grey continued, "Okay, on the count of three we'll jump, just don't forget to take a deep breath."

I nodded and squeezed his hand tighter. If Grey had asked me to do this with him a week ago, or even a few days prior, I would have said no. I was nervous, but somehow holding his hand and being with him made me feel like maybe it would be okay. Maybe it would be just like the dancing, like he said. I felt warm, and his touch comforted me enough for me to take the chance.

Grey started counting. "One. Two." I tightened my grip around his hand and inhaled a giant breath of air. "Three. Jump!"

We leaped off the dock. At first, I felt the cold shock of the water's embrace, but it faded after I was completely submerged into the water. Grey held my hand tightly, but I still held my breath as I looked around. It was as if I was surrounded by the blue sky, nearly floating in the air. No matter how hard my feet searched for the ground, it wasn't there.

There were small schools of petite fish, swimming together, and long plants with yellowish-green leaves that swayed back and forth with the waves of the water. They soothed my skin. I was so mesmerized by this world that I almost forgotten that I needed to swim up for air. I motioned my other hand towards my neck for Grey to see. He nodded and grabbed me closer. He kicked his legs and feet, and swam both of us up for air.

As our heads popped up above the water, my fingers clawed into him, tightly holding onto him so I wouldn't actually sink.

"It's okay. I've got you. I've got you," he said.

His words calmed my shaking nerves. I still firmly clung to him, but I did loosen a lot of my grip. He held me with one hand, and treaded water with the other. My nose was near his neck. He smelled of wood fire. He had always smelled of wood fire, but this time I was drawn to it.

"So, what did you think?" he asked.

"Not bad."

"Really? Just not bad?"

"Yeah." I grinned.

He smiled back.

"Still want to learn how to swim?" Grey asked. "Like I said, I won't let you drown."

I smiled at him. "I know. I trust you."

"Well, then. Lesson one: Seeing who can hold their breath the longest."

"You're on."

"On three. One…two…three."

We both took a deep breath and went back down.

We stayed in the water for hours, jumping, splashing, swimming… well, at least my attempt at swimming. We were finally out of the lake when evening fell, sitting next to each other on a fallen log at a campfire. Its orange flames created soothing crackles and pops into the air and a slight orange glow across Grey's face. I couldn't help but let out a little smile. I placed a couple of loose strands of hair that fell to the side of my face back, behind my ear and looked off at the shore. The sun was setting on the lake, with tints of blue and pink from the sky.

"So, that wasn't too bad," Grey said.

"Very funny." I looked back at Grey.

"Hey, a few more lessons and I'm sure that you'll be able to float, someday," he teased.

"Oh, keep laughing, because I assure you that my swimming skills are just about as good as your fighting skills."

"You wish!" He smiled.

"Oh, yeah. I will whip your ass any day, any time."

"Oh, could you now?"

"Uh huh. Just name the time and the place."

"How about right here, right now," Grey suggested.

"Okay, then."

"Do it," he said.

"You start."

"Oh, I have to start?"

"You suggested it."

"Alright, fine." He grabbed me closer and began tickling me on the sides of my stomach. I started pushing him away, unable to contain my laughter. I had leaned too far back, and began to fall backwards, only for my hand to be caught by Grey's hand. "See? Now, what would you do without me?" He asked, grinning.

"You're ridiculous." I smiled.

"Well, you—" he leaned forward towards me, but soon lost his balance as well. We both fell.

Grey landed off to the side, right next to me. I turned my face towards his, bursting into laughter. "Good job," I said, sarcastically.

"Very funny."

"Good, because I thought so."

He turned his face towards mine and for a moment our eyes locked. I could feel my cheeks turning red. I was becoming nervous, a weird kind of nervous. A nervousness that I couldn't quite describe or put into words, but at the same time it felt good. Really good. His emerald eyes shined, and I was drawn to him even more.

What's wrong with me?

I shook my head and turned it away.

"So yeah," I said, very awkwardly.

"Yeah, we should probably get back before it's too late. We don't want to run into any unexpected trouble or anything," Grey said.

"Right. We probably can't um, afford any more trouble."

We both stood up, me avoiding eye contact as he smothered the fire with dirt.

"That should do it," he said.

I could see him looking at me with the corner of my eye. Of course, I was looking off to the side. Nerves fluttered inside of my stomach, and I grabbed my left palm with my right hand up to my face. Why was it so warm?

"I'll race you."

"What?" I faced him.

"Rematch for last time," he said.

"Oh yeah, because I did let you catch me."

"Prove once and for all who the faster man or woman is," Grey said.

"Alright, but no magic."

"As long as there is no telekinesis."

"Deal!"

"Deal!"

We shook hands, and Grey started running.

"Jerk," I mumbled.

I began to run after him.

Towards the edge of the forest, the air was filled with the scent of smoke and burning wood. What had started as a friendly race had turned into a straight dash back to the cottage. When we reached the edge of the woods, and were only twenty feet from the cottage, we saw shattered glass from the windows. The wood from the porch was broken and charred with black marks, with smoke gently rising from it. The chairs from the inside had been thrown into the lawn with their legs scattered in the grass.

Johnny was pinned up against the wall on the side of the cottage by two sorcerers. He was held up by the collar by one, while the other dangled a dagger right beside his right cheek. His eyes were closed. His face was cocked to the side. And his mouth was shut, with blood already flowing down its corner.

The men were shrouded in dark cloaks, and their faces hidden by their hoods. All I could see were their outlines. They were tall, meeting Johnny in height. They were also wide and broad in shoulders.

"Johnny," I whispered.

I was stunned. For a few moments I stayed frozen there, until I ultimately decided that we had to help. This was his home, and he had been so kind. I motioned forward, but Grey grabbed my hand and pulled me off to the side, down into a bush.

"What are you doing? He's your friend. We have to help him," I whispered.

I propped back up, but Grey quickly pulled me back down.

"No, we can't." His voice was calm, yet drowning in sadness.

"What do you mean, we can't? He's your friend!"

"He'll be okay. We'll be doing him more harm than good if we show ourselves. Once they believe that we're not here, they'll leave. If they see us, we're dead, including Johnny for aiding us. Besides those men aren't official soldiers or anything. They're not wearing badges. They actually just look like more bunters."

"You said before that more would come looking for us?"

"Shhh! And yes, but again, they don't know that we're here."

I looked out at Johnny. He was still against the wall. His head was turned away from the men as they continued to manhandle him. The one with the dagger used the blade to nip a line into his cheek. My eyes watered for him, and for being unable to help.

"No matter," said one of the bunters. He pulled out a slender wooden rod with his bronze hand and held it up straight into the air.

"Shit! A wand!" Grey whispered.

"What's wrong?" I asked.

"Nothing, just hold onto me."

"What?"

Grey pointed at the rod. "That's a wand. It's a magic detector. It uses magic to detect the heat energy of magic in other sorcerers or magical creatures or items."

"Is he going to find us?"

"Hopefully this works," he mumbled.

"What?" I asked, sensing the concern in his voice.

"Nothing." His tone softened. "Don't worry. It will be fine." His mouth smiled, despite the worry in his eyes. He wrapped his arms around me and said, "Just hold onto me."

I placed my arms around him.

"*Glaecias,*" Grey said.

I felt a wisp of cold air touch my fingertips. It travelled through my hands, into my arms, and into my chest, where it continued to disperse throughout my entire body. I looked at Grey, and saw that his skin was beginning to turn into a blue tint. I glanced down at my arm. It was also turning the same color. Our body heat was vanishing, and breaths turned to thick and heavy smoke, as if it were winter. As my body became colder, I could feel myself losing energy, and my eyes started to become heavy. I laid my head on Grey's shoulder. I tried to remain still, but my body shivered.

"Don't worry. It will be over soon," he said.

I closed my eyes, yet trying to hold onto the little consciousness that I had left. Cries and screams emerged from the cottage. Grey tugged me, holding me closer. At first faint, the pitter-patter of footsteps grew louder as it approached us. When the sound reached its peak, it stopped. There was only silence. A few moments passed. The leaves from the bush had opened, and the light from the sky had shown through. "So, this is where you've been hiding," a foreign voice spoke.

And then everything went dark.

KING ZENTOS

"Are you fuckin' serious!?"

"Bradin, I can explain!"

"Johnny, double check that all of the windows and doors are closed. We don't need any accidental eavesdroppers."

"Mmm," I groaned as I slowly started to open eyes. I was in a bed, lying underneath a blue blanket. Cautiously, I sat up, and saw that I was once again in Grey's bedroom. According to the bright light outside the window next to his bed, it was morning. Like the day before, the room had a wooden desk and chair, a rug, and of the course the bed. All of which were here yesterday. It was untouched.

Grey must have carried me back here. Did the bunters from the night before just not get this room? How did it look so normal?

I was still a little dazed when I began to wake up and listen to the loud chatter of three voices coming from the other side of the bedroom door. I recognized Grey and Johnny's voices, but not the third. Wait, no... It was the foreign voice that I had heard while Grey and I were in the bush, right before...

"Grey, what the Hell is wrong with you!?" the strange voice shouted.

I got up and crept to the door. I cracked it open to see Grey, Johnny, and the stranger, all standing in the living room near the kitchen. He appeared to be another teen, but older, maybe even in his early twenties. He was similar to Grey in both stature and height. His face was similar to Johnny's, yet he had straight, dirty blonde hair, instead of brown hair. His hair swooped over to the side, barely touching his light gray eyes. This must have been Bradin.

He stood right next to Johnny, with his back turned against counter, and his front sternly facing Grey. Johnny had a few bruises along his neck and some cuts along his face, but he appeared to be okay. I let out a sigh of relief, remembering how I last saw him. I looked around the living room for signs of a fight, but everything seemed normal. The furniture was no longer broken, and each piece had been put neatly back in their place. The walls and floors were clean. It was like nothing had even happened yesterday.

How was that possible? Maybe magic was even more clever than I had thought?

"Bradin, she's still asleep. You might wake her up," Grey pleaded.

"Good! Because she should probably be a part of this conversation too! I swear, Grey. Do you ever take anything seriously!? No, no you don't! You're too busy playing house to…ugh, my Perencia…I can't even form the words!"

"I'm sorry. I didn't mean for this happen. I didn't know that they would come looking for us here."

"You know how fast rumors travel throughout this country. I even heard the rumors of a sorcerer boy with a psychic girl together in Brunsick while I was in Lopidus. But who knew that they were about you!" Bradin yelled. "Johnny literally could have been killed. You realize that, right? Or been captured or tortured or who knows what! You're lucky that didn't happen."

"Or worse," Johnny said.

Bradin immediately turned to him and shouted, "Shut Up!"

Johnny looked down at the floor as Bradin turned back to Grey.

Bradin continued: "But, he's right. People literally disappear from just openly saying or thinking the wrong thing against the Crown, let alone if they think you're hiding some type of information from it. You know that! You know all of this! Grey, I just…what were you thinking?"

Grey was unable hold eye contact with Bradin. He titled his head slightly off to the side and down towards the floor. "If you want us out—"

"Ugh. Don't be so dramatic," Bradin interrupted. "I could never actually kick you out. You're family. You know that."

Bradin glanced towards the door. I ducked. "The girl, does she know?" he asked.

Know what? I wondered. I waited a few seconds before I popped my head back up to see that they were now all facing each other.

Grey shook his head.

Bradin sighed. "Grey."

"I know. I was going to tell her, but then I kept putting it off. Honestly, we were just having so much fun that even the thought of coming back to reality seemed—"

"Yeah?" Bradin asked.

Grey sighed. "I don't know."

"Grey?"

"Yeah."

"Do you care about this girl?"

"Of course, I do."

"Then you need to tell her the truth, because you're not only putting all of our lives on the line, you are especially putting her life in danger," Bradin said.

"Okay, I'll tell her," Grey agreed.

"Good. Do it today, or I will." Bradin turned. He took a few steps forward, then stopped. He looked back at Grey. "This shit got all of our parents killed. Remember that. This is not our war anymore."

"I couldn't just leave her, Bradin. She's—"

"I know what she is," Bradin interrupted. "Keep playing this game and you're going to get yourself killed. Just tell her."

Tell me what?

There was a somber silence between the three of them, until Bradin looked over at Johnny and said, "Come on. Let's go."

"Huh? What? Where are we going?" Johnny asked.

"Into town. I need help keeping an eye on the pumpkins and selling them at the market," Bradin said.

"You can't put a protector spell on them, or anything?"

"Suck it up, Johnny," Bradin said as he headed out of the kitchen.

Johnny glanced over at Grey, who shrugged his shoulders.

"You know that there are too many counter spells to count, nowadays. Besides, we're going to need the money. The tree barks have already gotten thicker than normal, there are flowers still trying to bloom, and a lot of the leaves are still on the branches." Bradin turned his head, looking back at Johnny. "It's going to be a longer and harsher winter than most. Not to mention that we barely afford the taxes as it is. I don't want to leave anything to chance. I will meet you outside, right by the barn door. *Transmedo!*"

Bradin disappeared.

"Yup. Of course, this happens." Johnny looked over at Grey. He was staring down at the floor, with his hands in his pockets. Johnny placed his hand on Grey's shoulder. "It will be fine, Grey. You know how Bradin is. *Transmedo!*"

Johnny vanished.

Grey looked over at the door. I ducked. I popped my head up a few moments later. He stood a little longer before walking away.

What is he not telling me? We've spent so much time together, now and he is still keeping secrets...

I waited a few minutes before quietly walking out into the living room. And to my surprise, on the counter that separated the living room from the kitchen, there was a silver, heart shaped locket staring back at me. It sparkled its engraved swirls and flowers. I gasped.

It looked like the same locket that I had lost when I had first met Grey. How was that even possible? I mean, how could it have gotten here? It held the same silver chain, and it missed the same front piece.

I walked around the counter and into the kitchen to further examine it. Carefully, my fingers began to graze over it. Just as before, when I had first found myself teleported into an underground tunnel from its touch, I had now found myself teleported to a different location. I was not in a tunnel. I was in the middle of a forest. It was dark, but the sky lit by a full moon. I stood in a small circle, surrounded trees, bushes, and other greenery, that were all casted in shadow. The air was quiet, almost unnerving. I looked around to make sure that this quietness was not the result of some predator suddenly eyeing me, closing in. There was no sign of anyone. Not even the woman from the cinder tunnel was present.

I sighed in relief. I did not want to see her. The mere memory of her presence gave me chills. I shivered at the thought of her. Her body laid as still as a corpse in a dark hooded cap, but her lips moved. *"Promise Me,"* she whispered.

I shook her image of out of my head. *Why did I ever touch that locket?* It was cold. I placed my hands in my pockets.
What the—?

There was something metallic in the right pocket. I pulled it out to find the locket.

"Hello, Cassandra."

I gasped. My ears perked up. It was the voice from the locket, except this time it came from behind, and it was louder and a little deeper. I stood still. The edge between the bottom of my neck and collar bone stiffened. I clenched the locket tightly in my hand. From the corner of my eye, I could only see a shadow of a figure who hadn't been there just a moment before. My heart sped. I cautiously placed the locket back in my pocket. I turned around to face the figure.

"Or do you prefer to be called, 'Alex'?" The figure stepped forward into the light. "Either way, it is enchanting to finally make your acquaintance."

I squinted my eyes. "You're the sorcerer from the painting in the tavern!"

The pitch of my voice rose in astonishment.

It was the tavern that Grey and I had first gone to in order to hide from the soldiers after he stole the dress. He was tall, blue-eyed, and angular in face. He was an older gentleman, with long blonde hair slicked back that touched past his shoulders. In fact, the color of his hair was so light that it nearly looked white. He wore white gloves and dark blue robes with red trimmings and buttons in contrast to his pale skin.

"My, you are a lot sharper than your family gives you credit for." He took another step forward, but I took a step back.

"Who are you and what do you want?" I asked.

He chuckled. "My child, I'm sure that you've heard of me."

"Try me."

"My name is Zentos."

"You!? No, stay back! Get away from me!" I yelled. I lifted my hands up in defense. "I don't know what you want, but you're not going to take me!"

"Do not be alarmed," Zentos said.

I shook my head as I motioned back. I turned around to run. However, only a few moments passed until Zentos teleported himself right in front of me, stopping me in my path. I jumped back.

"I am not here to harm you, Child," he said.

"You sent bounty hunters to kidnap me!"

"Yes, I hired those men to bring you home. Only, I had no idea that they would use such barbaric tactics. They were never instructed to do so, and for that I assure you that they will be thoroughly punished."

"Wha… What do you mean home? What are you talking about?"

"Your birth home. The home that was stolen from you by the kidnappers that you call Mom and Dad."

"No. That doesn't make any sense."

"You must have wondered why you've always felt different from them. How you don't even look like them?"

"No, I have my mother's freckles and my great grandfather's dark hair."

"Ah, yes. That is what they told you, isn't it? Your so-called mother is not the only person in the world to carry such a trait, and neither is it unusual to have a dark mane. But really think about it. Do you actually see yourself in them?"

Of course, I did. He was lying. He had to be lying. I refused to believe him.

"Those high cheekbones of yours, and then of course your eyes."

"What is with everyone's fixation on my eyes!?"

"Oh, so Grey has not told you either, has he?"

"How do you know—"

"Only the offspring of both magic and psychic blood can have golden eyes."

"What!? No! That's impossible!" I took a step back and shook my head in disbelief.

"Is it? You're a sorceress, Cassandra."

"No. You're just trying to trick me. Don't you think I would know if I was a sorceress or not?"

"Which reminds me." He waved his hand and said, *"Capara microchip!"*

Immediately, pain started to shoot through my left shoulder. I screamed as I grabbed it with my right hand. "What are you trying to do to me!?"

He stood patiently in silence.

From my shoulder and through my sleeve flew out a tiny square microchip, landing in the sorcerer's hand. Most of the pain had stopped, but I continued to hold my shoulder to prevent the small droplets of blood from seeping onto my skin and into my sleeve.

"These devices are quite useful, aren't they? Unless placed in the wrong hands. Coincidentally, they are the same devices that the psychic government uses to both track and suppress the flow of magical energy in their prisoners. Intriguing how it ended up inside of you," he said.

I gazed down at the ground. How was this possible? No, there had to be some type of logical explanation. My parents wouldn't do this. They wouldn't lie about something this bad.

"You see, I have not come here to hurt you. I have only wanted to help you from the moment I found you. Have I not warned you about those people that took you, guided you out of that prison that they kept you in, and then told you the truth? It was only when we got separated that I was unable to further help you, Cassandra," he said.

I looked up at him, still speechless. I wasn't sure what to say, what to think, or what to do. My mind went blank.

He continued: "Come with me, and I will personally show you and teach you about your true lineage. I knew your parents very well, especially your father. It would only be right for me to teach you of him, and of the true magic that you possess."

I clutched my shoulder more.

"The choice is yours. *Imperium!*"

Intense electrifying energy struck me. It surged through my core, feeling intense, yet exhilarating. It was warm and soothing, yet made my heart race. My limbs felt lighter, more agile, but stronger. It was as if I had been given a surge of super human strength and a strong rush of adrenaline.

Zentos snapped his fingers, and it was gone.

I stared down at my hands as I brought them in closer towards my face.

What just happened?

"Take all of the time that you want to decide. If you need me, use the locket. As always, the choice is yours," he said.

My surroundings darkened even more, and then everything began to disappear.

I closed my eyes, but when I re-opened them, I was lying on the kitchen floor back at the cottage. I sat up on my knees. Was all of that just a dream? I touched my left shoulder with my hand and saw that same tear in my sleeve, and the tiny droplets of clotted blood around my skin. I placed both hands in front of me, staring down at them. Behind me was a stone fireplace. I turned towards it, glancing back and forth at my hands and it. If what he said was true, then I had to test it, right? But I didn't know any spells. Well, there was one. One that I'd heard multiple times. I stretched out my arms, with my palms facing the fireplace and spoke: *"Detra Arma!"*

Nothing happened.

These were the same words that I had heard Grey recite over and over again.

I took a deep breath, closed my eyes, and with all my might, I repeated: *"DETRA ARMA!"*

A yellow flash of light shot from my palms into the fireplace. The force of the blast threw me back into the lower cabinets and caused the dishes hanging overhead to shake. "Ow!"

It was true. They lied to me. They all lied to me. My parents. Grey. Hannah? *Did you know too?* My head spun.

"Cass, is that you?" Grey called.

How could they all lie to me?

"Cass?" Grey walked into the kitchen and saw me sitting on the floor.

"Are you okay?" he asked.

I glared up at him.

"So, this might be a bad time, but there is something that I need to tell you—" he began.

"You lied to me," I interrupted.

"What?" he asked.

I stood up, facing him. "You knew this entire time why everyone was after me. That I wasn't just a—" Then, it clicked. "That day when we first met, and you called me 'Cassie'—"

"Cass."

"Oh my gosh, I'm such an idiot! It was obvious that you knew! That you knew what was going on this entire time and you lied to me just like everyone else!"

"I can explain."

"I trusted you! You kept asking me to trust you and then I finally did." My face turned red from the heat that brewed inside it.

"Cass…"

"No! I will never make that mistake again!"

"I was going to tell you." Grey took a step forward, but I took a step back.

"Bullshit! When were you going to tell me, huh!? When!? Only one person bothered to tell me the truth and he—" I cut myself off.

"Bradin? Wait, no. Bradin and Johnny are still out and they haven't come back yet. Who told you?"

I opened my lips, but closed them again.

"Cass?"

Immediately, Bradin and Johnny teleported themselves into the kitchen. All of the curtains unwrapped themselves, covering the windows, and the clicking of the porch door locking shut echoed through the darkness. "There are two people nearby looking for the girl, a man and a woman," Bradin said.

"That's easy enough. We can hide or go somewhere and blend in the crowd. It'll be fine," Grey said.

"Grey, they have a sketch, a very detailed sketch." Bradin turned to me. "And the way they described you, it seemed as if they knew you."

"No, I can't handle this right now!" I said, frantically. The sketch. The tracking device. It had to be my parents.

"Cass, we'll figure this out," Grey said as he approached me.

I stepped back. "Do not touch me!"

I ran back into the bedroom and locked the door.

Knock! Knock!

"Cass, come on. We can work this out!" Grey said on the other side of the door.

I ran up to the window and climbed onto its sill. When I tried to open it, it was locked. I aimed my palms at the latch and recited the spell again. Yellow light traveled from my palms and to the latch, breaking it. I opened the window and jumped out of it.

I ran back into the woods, my feet feeling as though they were moving on their own.

"Cass!" Grey's voice appeared from behind.

Shit!

He must have followed me out. If only I had the speed or the strength to move faster. That desire reminded me of the adrenaline rush that I was given when I was with Zentos. The tiny hairs on my skin stood up at the very thought of that feeling.

I levitated the locket from my pocket and into my hand. I held it tightly and whispered, "Zentos."

The wind picked up, and a blue light in the form of a single vertical line appeared in front of me. I slowed down and stopped to stare at the light.

"Cass," Grey caught up to me and stopped, as well. He stood speechless as he watched Zentos step forward from the light.

Zentos turned to me. "You called?"

He glanced over at Grey. "Ah. Young Greyson, nice to see you again."

Grey's eyes glared and narrowed themselves into Zentos' eyes. He scowled and his face turned red as he clenched his fits together.

"Huh," Zentos continued, calmly. He looked around the forest. "So, this is the area in which you have been residing." He turned his attentions back to Grey. "Tell me. Are your friends also close?"

"You leave them out of this or I SWEAR I WILL—!" Grey began.

"ALEX NO!"

"AHHH!" I screamed. My hands went up to my ears at the piercing sound of my father's voice inside my head. I leaned forward, with my face and shoulders titled towards the ground.

"Cass, are you okay?"

"ALEX!"

My eyes widened.

Mom?

I turned my head and saw both of my parents quickly approaching from the right. My breath stopped. *They found me.* The words echoed in my head. Words that I had longed to say weeks ago, yet in this moment only filled me with dread.

I gasped, remembering to breathe. I stood up, staring straight at my father. He pulled out a cylindrical object from his pocket. It looked metallic, but I couldn't completely make it out. He stretched it out in front of him, and three red lasers shot from its end. Both Grey and I jumped back. They went past us, generating wind as they flew by. I looked at Zentos. He stood tall and calm, and he actually smirked.

Zentos, not phased by the lasers inches from his face, dispersed them with the flick of his wrist. My mouth gaped open in surprise. I had never seen anyone do that.

"Alex!"

I looked back at my parents. They were now only yards away.

"GET AWAY FROM HIM!" Mom cried. Her voice was both shaky and frantic.

"Alex, step back!" Dad's voice was cautious. "This sorcerer is very dangerous. Come here, now!"

"No." I began to shake my head, and stepped back further away from my father.

"Alex, please!" Mom cried out in desperation. Her eyes were glistening from tears.

"Why am I part magic!? Why have you never told me?" I asked.

"Sweetheart, this is my fault. We should have told you a long time ago, but this sorcerer, like your father is saying, is very dangerous. Please, I beg you. You cannot trust him or anything that he says. All he will do is manipulate and hurt you. Please," she extended her hand. "Just come with us now."

"He's the only person that has told me the truth. There is no possible way that you are my real parents," I said.

I stepped back further.

"You stole me, didn't you?" My voice was soft, yet started to increase in pitch, and cracked from my growing anguish. How could they have done this to me? For years they lied to me, years! They were the true manipulators.

"No, Alex, that is not what happened. We can explain," Mom said.

"Then, why do I have magic!?" I asked.

Her mouth opened, but no words came out. She only looked at me with saddened eyes.

"ANSWER ME!" I shouted.

I looked down at my hands. I held them out right in front of me, with my palms open towards myself. "Please," I whispered.

Tears streamed down my cheeks. I closed my eyes and balled my hands into fists. "Is that why you locked me away all this time? Why I've always felt so different? And why you even CHIPPED ME!?"

"Alex—"

"No." I opened my eyes and looked back at my parents. "Who are you? How could you do this to me?" I asked.

"Alex, we clothed you. We fed you. And we love you," Dad said. "You are our child, despite what this sorcerer, or what anyone else says. You are mine. Be angry at me, not your mother. I was too strict on you. I was just trying to protect you. Everything that we have done has been to protect you, specifically from this sorcerer. That is why we've been hiding."

He pointed at Zentos. "He has been trying to find you since the moment that you were born!"

His voice became soft. "We should have told you the truth a long time ago. Come, please."

"Heartfelt speech. And an intriguing accusation from the person that kidnapped her. However, you never answered her original question. Why is she half magic?" Zentos asked.

"Stay out of this!" Dad yelled, his face turning red.

He turned to me. I stood there, frozen.

What do I do?

"Alex." Dad gestured his hand towards me.

Grey stood in between Zentos and I. He glared up at Zentos and said, "You're not taking her. I will fight you until I'm purple, blue, or whatever comes of me, but I will never let you have her."

He put his hands up, with his palms facing Zentos.

My entire body started to become numb. My arms slightly lowered, and I was left utterly confused. I still loved my parents, despite their lies. But they were not my real parents. Had they stolen me? Why had they chipped me? Kept me a prisoner? If they hated sorcerers, and I had magic, did they hate me too? Is that why I was their prisoner?

I couldn't trust them, or Grey, or anyone. I was alone, except…

"Alex, please this is serious." Dad clenched his fist. "We're taking you back whether you like it or not!"

He began to run towards me.

"No!" I snapped. Instantly, a yellow ball of light shot from the palm of my hand and went past my father.

He stopped. His eyes widened and he turned back. "Gabby, move!" he yelled.

Mom turned to run. But the blast still hit her full force. She let out a piercing scream as the spell made contact with her body, before falling limply to the ground.

I gasped. My hands covered my mouth as I whispered, "Mommy."

What have I done?

Dust from the ground filled the air. "Gabby!" Dad yelled again.

"Mommy, I'm so sorry," I said as tears ferociously rushed down my cheeks. My heart was throbbing.

Mom laid on the ground holding her right arm with her left hand. Dad knelt down at her side, attempting to grab her, but she said: "No. It's alright. I'm alright. It will heal. You have to get Alex."

Zentos chuckled.

Dad looked up at him, glaring.

Grey ran over to my mother. However, Dad stood up on guard in between them.

"It's okay. I won't hurt her." Grey held up both of his hands cautiously in the air. "I am the son of Lena Bracksworth, from the resistance. Zentos is my enemy, too. I can make sure that she is okay."

Dad gave Grey a nod. Did they know each other? Did Dad know Grey's parents? What were they talking about? Dad turned to face Zentos.

"I'm not going to let you go after my child," Dad said.

All of the voices around me became faint, until I could no longer hear them. Instead, I only heard the sound of my mother's scream, of my parents' lies, and of Grey's deception. I looked forward, but before I even realized it, my feet had already started running away.

I ran as fast as I could through the forest, refusing to look back. I just wanted to forget. I could hear the sounds of explosions and blasts behind me. I pushed myself to run further and further, until I heard nothing.

Out of breath, I stopped at an old willow tree. I nearly collapsed forward into its thick trunk. I stretched out my arms and pressed my hands against its rugged exterior. I took a few deep breaths, then turned my back against the trunk. I sunk onto the ground and looked down at my trembling hands. Slowly, I wrapped my arms around myself, while pulling my knees closer. Although the tears had slowed, I could still hear the sound of my mother's scream screeching through my ears. I placed my hands on top of my ears, as if I could block out her screams from continuously repeating in my memory. I closed my eyes and sunk my forehead into my knees.

I felt the wind graze the top of my head, and heard the rustle of the leaves in the trees and bushes. I opened my eyes and looked up. There was something in the bush a few feet across from me. Something moving.

I sat still, quietly listening. My hands went to my side. My fingers slowly laced themselves around the handle of the dagger I still had at my waist. The bush stopped moving, and out hopped a tiny brown rabbit. I sighed in relief and leaned my back against the tree.

I pulled the locket out from my pocket, tracing the silver chain with the tips of my fingers. He was the only one that told me the truth.

Regardless of my parents' reasoning, they had lied to me my entire life. I felt so different about them now. A feeling that I thought could never be undone. Deep down, I knew that it was always strange that I did not look like them, but they always found a way to explain it away.

Who are, or were, my real parents?
Are they still alive?
What happened to them?
What were they like?
Why was I given up or taken?

I held up the body of the locket close to my face. I stared at it until I finally said the word: "Zentos."

The wind began to pick up. It touched the ground, spiraling in front of me as if it were a miniature tornado. In its center glowed a bright white light. It grew until it engulfed the spiraling wind.

"Cassandra," it whispered.

Cautiously, I stood up.

"Cassandra," it said, again.

I gazed down at the locket. I still held it in my hand. My eyes went back to the light. Like a trance, my feet began to slowly walk towards the light. When I reached it, I extended my other hand to touch it. It felt warm and soothing. As I extended my hand further into the light, it had seemly disappeared. I pulled it back, and it appeared again.

"I've heard of these," I whispered.

I took a deep breath and stepped through the portal. I entered into a gray stone corridor. It was dimly lit, with flaming torches along its walls for light. The tile floor was dark and coldly. It was quiet, extremely quiet. The portal that stood behind me had vanished, and in its stead stood the shadow of a tall, husky, hooded figure. The outline of its shoulders were muscular. He was wrapped in a dark cloak and hood.

He withdrew a dagger from the inside of his cloak, and placed its blade to the left inside of my lower back.

I froze. Blood trickled down my limb, and my strength slowly began to dwindle. The locket slipped through my fingers. The sound of its metal echoed throughout the corridor as it hit the floor. My body trembled from both the weakness and the pressing pain until it could no longer hold itself up, then I collapsed onto the floor.

"Welcome home, Mutt."

I laid still in a puddle of my own blood. The chill of the floor seeped through my clothes and into my skin. I shivered at first, but then I was only numb. I stared up at the stone walls until my eyes no longer had the strength to keep themselves open.

"Plan executed. Inform His Majesty of the good news. We've got her."

Footsteps emerged into the tunnel. They approached until everything became quiet.

EPILOGUE

"Your Grace? Your Grace?"
"Huh? Wait, what?" I ask.

My eyes open and circle around the room until they eventually land on Lord Edgewater. I am back in the wardrobe. Lord Edgewater smiles at me with such excitement and joy in his eyes. It is quite the contrast to my nerves.

"Oh, my apologies, Lord Edgewater. I must have gotten lost in my thoughts," I say.

"Shall we?" Lord Edgewater gestures an open hand towards me. "We have all been waiting a long time for this moment."

"Of course." I weakly smile.

"Isabelle." I nod my head down towards the letters that I still hold in my hand.

Isabelle perks up. She runs and fetches a large envelope. After she hands it to me, I place the letters in the envelope and hand it back to her. She knows where to put it.

I turn my attentions back to Lord Edgewater. I step down from the platform and extend my left hand towards his. He gently catches it and begins to escort me out of the room. As we walk, I cannot help but think about that day. That day in which I laid nearly dead on that cold tile floor. I shudder, and my back flinches as it remembers the blade penetrating into my skin. However, just like this new adventure that I am about to embark on, that tale is not over. No. It has only just begun.

www.ingramcontent.com/pod-product-compliance
Lightning Source LLC
LaVergne TN
LVHW091546070526
838199LV00024B/561/J